Caitlin's eyes caught the calendar hanging below the kitchen clock. Today's date was ringed. It was important. *February the fourteenth. St. Valentine's Day.* The day for lovers to declare themselves. A day to concentrate on romance.

Caitlin tore off the offending page and crushed it in her hand. She threw the crumpled wad of paper into the bin. If only she could get rid of her unrequited love for David as easily....

EMMA DARCY nearly became an actress until her fiancé declared he preferred to attend the theater *with* her. She became a wife and mother. Later, she took up oil painting—unsuccessfully, she remarks. Then she tried architecture, designing the family home in New South Wales. Next came romance writing—"the hardest and most challenging of all the activities," she confesses.

Books by Emma Darcy

HARLEQUIN PRESENTS PLUS
1632—THE SHINING OF LOVE
1679—IN NEED OF A WIFE

HARLEQUIN PRESENTS
1536—AN IMPOSSIBLE DREAM
1659—A WEDDING TO REMEMBER

Don't miss any of our special offers. Write to us at the following address for information on our newest releases.

Harlequin Reader Service
U.S.: 3010 Walden Ave., P.O. Box 1325, Buffalo, NY 14269
Canadian: P.O. Box 609, Fort Erie, Ont. L2A 5X3

EMMA DARCY

Burning With Passion

Harlequin Books

TORONTO • NEW YORK • LONDON
AMSTERDAM • PARIS • SYDNEY • HAMBURG
STOCKHOLM • ATHENS • TOKYO • MILAN
MADRID • WARSAW • BUDAPEST • AUCKLAND

To Scott Brodie, our hero on many occasions.
Our thanks for his diplomacy, tact, understanding
and caring.

ISBN 0-373-11721-3

BURNING WITH PASSION

Copyright © 1995 by Emma Darcy.

First North American Publication 1995.

CHAPTER ONE

LOVING David Hartley was like dancing with the devil. There was no telling where it would lead to, there was hell to pay for it, yet the temptation to go on with the dance was well nigh irresistible.

For Caitlin Ross, there was little of her life that did not revolve around David Hartley. Yet she was no closer to the quintessential man than she had been four months ago when she had been offered the job as his personal assistant.

Her promotion from personal assistant in the office to personal assistant in the bedroom had been extraordinarily rapid by any standard. Caitlin hadn't said no to him because he simply hadn't given her time to say anything. He had taken her over in the same way he did any competitor, company or conglomerate. It was breathtaking stuff.

It was only after they had made love for the first time that the situation became confused. Caitlin had discovered there were two distinctive features to David's personality. The first was that he never referred to his family or his background; the second was that he had a very strict rule against the fraternisation of management and employees in sexual liaisons. He made no exceptions to this rule, apart from breaking it himself.

Caitlin reasoned that he needed someone attuned to his business life, someone with whom he could talk about the things that were important to him, someone who understood. Caitlin could supply that in a way no other woman could. She was closest to him. She loved being closest to him. But it was nowhere near as close as she wanted to be.

In far too many ways, David had made himself an island complete and entire in himself. There were gleams of the person he could be, shining through isolated chinks in his armour, but they were few and far between.

Only in bed did his control slip. When they were finished with their lovemaking he donned it again like impenetrable armour. When he left her, it was as though she no longer existed.

Caitlin had watched him do it again this morning. She wanted to fight it but she didn't know how. It made her feel threatened and defeated. She couldn't understand why he wanted, desired her so much, and then shut her out of the closeness she was sure he felt with her in the intimacy of making love.

He strode back into her bedroom.

He was freshly showered and shaved and unashamedly naked. She felt her innermost muscles spasm in response simply to seeing him like this. His body was perfectly proportioned and powerful. He was the ultimate male animal in his prime, although no longer primed for the passion he had already spent some twenty minutes ago. Burn-out for him. Caitlin wanted more. Much more than this.

He looked revitalised after his shower. He always did. His straight black hair was combed back, wet and shiny; his olive skin stretched glowingly over high cheekbones, a cleanly cut jawline and strong nose; his dark, cobalt-blue eyes were lit with purpose for the day ahead of him. A man of command, who drove forward unswervingly, touching everyone within his ambit.

Caitlin fiercely wished she could exercise some influence over his thinking. That had not proved possible. Yet.

He raised a quizzical eyebrow at her as he reached for the shirt he had tossed on to her dressing-table stool last night. 'No coffee?'

Normally it was on the dressing-table, waiting for him, freshly brewed, black with one sugar. He drank it while he dressed. He never stayed to have breakfast with her. As far as Caitlin could discern, he didn't eat breakfast.

It was six-thirty now. He would be gone by six forty-five. That was the ritual. He never varied it. Caitlin wished he would.

'I don't feel like moving,' she answered his question on the missing coffee. It was the truth. It was also an act of rebellion.

The fractional tightening of David's lower lip indicated the message had been received and understood. Caitlin wondered if it would induce David to change his schedule. Would it drive him to making some coffee for himself, and for *her*? It would only delay him five or ten minutes at the most.

She waited expectantly to see his choice.

He continued dressing, shoving his arms into the sleeves of his shirt, doing up the cuff buttons. He made no move towards the kitchen. Caitlin tried to suppress the nervous flutter that descended to the pit of her stomach.

She had done everything in her power to spin out the dance as long as she could. She had been so careful not to make a false step that would contravene his rules, always fulfilling his needs as she saw them, polishing her role as the perfect partner for him, telling herself that holding David Hartley was worth any effort.

The strain was beginning to tell. The piper had to be paid for the effort she had put in, and the list of dues owed was becoming longer and longer.

Caitlin knew she risked losing him if she tried to change their relationship. After four months of going all his way, Caitlin also knew she was losing too much of herself. She could not let things remain as they were between them. Change was inevitable.

David shot her a sharp frown. 'Are you sick?' He was trying to find some explanation for her behaviour which fitted into his pattern of thinking.

'I've never felt healthier!' she answered, forcing him to think again, thoroughly peeved with his rigidly kept schedule.

She stretched languorously, provocatively, wondering if it was possible to tempt him back into bed with her. She watched his response through her thick dark lashes, her green eyes glimmering a sultry invitation. His firmly delineated mouth quirked into a sensual little smile as his gaze flicked over her naked breasts.

It was purely an accident of birth that her ribcage was high enough to give her a tiny waist. It had the effect of making her hips and breasts look more voluptuous than they were. Caitlin knew David found the arrangement fascinating, provocative and exciting.

There was a gleam of appreciation in his eyes. No desire. His hands moved down his shirt, buttoning it at a steady pace. No hesitation. No wavering. No change of mind, or heart, or inclination. He had had his fulfilment for the moment. He had no need for more. She doubted he ever gave consideration to the possibility that some of her needs were different from his.

Caitlin was deeply wounded by his ability to love her and leave her. The urge to jolt him into reappraisal mode was overwhelming. She realigned her body across the bed for full visual impact, levered herself up on one elbow, rummaged the long, layered mane of her tawny hair with her other hand, and eyed him with smouldering challenge.

'I don't want you to go,' she said quietly but firmly.

David rolled his eyes and threw a beseeching look towards the heavens. As his gaze was interrupted by the ceiling, there was no result to this supplicating action except to pique Caitlin somewhat more than she was already piqued.

He glanced pointedly at his watch and bent to pick up his underpants from the floor. 'I have a busy schedule to keep, Caitlin. You know that. You entered it in the diary.'

She watched him draw on the black silk briefs. They formed a tantalising pouch for his virility and emphasised the powerful muscularity of his thighs. He looked sexy. He was sexy. But Caitlin wanted more than sexiness from him. She wanted to know how important she was in his life.

'Please, David . . . couldn't you give me today? I'll make you happy.'

'I am happy. I'm delirious with happiness. Thank you for already making me so happy.'

To Caitlin's mind he didn't look the least bit happy. His words sounded sarcastic. She was quite certain he wasn't at all happy with the way things were developing between them.

'I want you to stay with me.'

Caitlin knew she was on very dangerous grounds with that plea. She was also probably wrong to put such a demand on him, but her need was acute. In a desperate attempt to interest him she pulled a long tress of her hair forward to dangle between her breasts, reminding him of the foreplay he enjoyed.

He gave her a sharp, penetrating look. 'Are you saying I didn't satisfy you?'

She flushed, unable to deny that he had brought her to a tumultuous climax. He was well aware of it, too. But, in a far more important sense than the purely physical, he didn't satisfy her. Caitlin wanted—needed—intimate contact with his innermost feelings.

'I want us to spend more time together,' she said, willing him to respond with some suggestion that would help make things better for her.

'We spent the night together,' he said drily. 'How many nights do you want?' He reached for his trousers.

Caitlin fought against a sense of worthlessness and failure. She knew that in David's mind nights were associated with sex. He wasn't getting the message at all.

'I want to talk to you. About something serious.'

'In another two hours we'll be in the office together. Isn't that serious enough?'

'It's not the same,' she retorted, hurt by his lack of understanding, knowing she was losing but too frustrated by his intransigent attitude to back off from the disagreement.

'You want more?'

'Yes.'

'What?'

'I'd very much like, just for once, for our pleasure and togetherness to come before your business.'

The act of rebellion was complete. Words had been spoken which could never be retrieved. The Rubicon was crossed. Caitlin waited to see what stormy waves she had stirred. The cobalt-blue eyes took on a wary, calculating look.

David never mixed business with pleasure. It was one of his rules. In the office, he was the boss, she was his assistant and amanuensis, and he never did or said anything to lead anyone to suspect they were lovers. That was private. It was personal. It was never to be revealed.

The two separate phases of his existence were divorced from one another. Caitlin couldn't help thinking the arrangement suited his convenience. She worked his hours. She was free when he was free. But business was business and nothing else was allowed to interfere with running that part of his life as he saw fit. Nothing!

'It wouldn't hurt to take one day off and spend it together,' she pressed.

'What would it achieve that we haven't already achieved?'

'It would be something spontaneous, unplanned.' She made one last attempt to get through to him. 'It would make me feel good.'

'I left my schooldays behind me a long time ago, Caitlin.'

He was downgrading her to 'petulant schoolgirl' status.

'You could cancel your appointments today. I'll make the excuses for you,' she pleaded.

'No.'

'You could come back to bed and hug and cuddle and kiss me.'

His look of disdain downgraded her from schoolgirl to child.

He tucked in his shirt, zipped up his trousers, then sat on the stool, stony-faced as he began to pull on his socks.

'Those are yesterday's socks,' said Caitlin with an uncharacteristic spurt of bitterness. 'You'll have to go home and change.'

'I know *that*,' he replied with some asperity.

She had invited him to leave a fresh set of clothes in her apartment for the times he stayed overnight. It would have saved him the trouble of going home to change. He would not have to rise so early. He could stay and have breakfast with her.

His reply had been succinct and dismissive. He wouldn't burden her with his dirty laundry.

He didn't burden her with anything. His only concession to practicality about their relationship was to keep a toothbrush, a shaving kit and a comb in her bathroom. To Caitlin it smacked of a clinical detachment from getting involved in any way except the obvious. She didn't like it.

It hurt.

It made her feel temporary.

She desperately wanted to feel special to him, more special than any woman he had been with before.

'Why don't you ever invite me to your home, David?' she asked, driven to wring some sign from him that she meant more than a pleasurable convenience and receptacle.

'It's easier for you if we stay here. You can do as you please and be answerable to no one,' he replied, not bothering to look up from tying the laces on his shoes.

Her convenience. That was a nice twist. In effect, she was kept excluded from his home life. Caitlin knew he lived at Lane Cove, not far from his business headquarters at Chatswood. Within the ambit of the northern suburbs of Sydney, it was no further away than her place at Wollstonecraft, but their intimacy was contained to her apartment.

Caitlin was chillingly conscious of how expedient this situation was if David chose to end their affair. No bothersome complications. He could simply walk out and never come back.

Her sense of insecurity with him deepened.

He rose from the stool, fully dressed apart from his tie and suitcoat. They had been discarded in her living-room. He would pick them up on his way out. His gaze skated over the long sprawl of her slender legs, paused at the deep indentation of her waist, skipped to the wild disarray of hair framing her face and shoulders, then fastened directly on her eyes. There was a dark, ruthless glint in his.

'I hope you find the energy to move yourself in good time to get to the office at nine, Caitlin. I wouldn't like to think you were taking advantage of your situation.'

It was a warning. Softly spoken, perfectly controlled, no direct threat involved, yet Caitlin's spine crawled with the sense of having stretched beyond what was acceptable to him. The protective urge to quickly backtrack was shrivelled by a flare of burning resentment.

Did she have no importance in his life apart from being an efficient secretary and a ready source of sexual satisfaction? It was the final insult. She had worked herself to boneless exhaustion for David Hartley.

'You have the sensitivity of a rhinoceros,' she muttered darkly, more to herself than to him.

'I'll let that remark pass and pretend you never said it,' he said testily.

'Big of you,' she complimented him.

The need to find out what she really meant to him surged through her with passionate intensity. Even if his heart was cold to her, his body wasn't. She must mean something more than just being a body.

She swung her legs off the bed with a lithe, feline grace that captured his attention. She lifted her arms and flicked back her hair as she stood up and turned to face him, knowing the action tilted the firm fullness of her breasts into greater prominence. Her nipples hardened as the desire to seduce raged with white-hot heat. She rolled her hips, sliding her thighs against each other as she walked towards him, a sensual smile curving her generous mouth.

He couldn't tear his eyes away from her.

His chest expanded. His shoulders squared with tension. His hands clenched. He was definitely unhappy. He was tempted. His mind warred against the stirring of his desire. He had a schedule to keep. He didn't allow anything to interfere with that. His face set with resolution but the glitter in his eyes had more to do with lust than determination. His feet stayed rooted to the floor. He didn't move forward.

'Is this the last time you want to see me like this?' Caitlin taunted.

'No,' he cried hoarsely.

'Stay with me. Hold me and cuddle me.'

'I'll be damned if I will.'

'You'll be damned if you don't.'

'I have the overseas delegation today.'

Caitlin knew she was being unreasonable but her need was great. 'Defer it until tomorrow.'

His mouth thinned in frustration.

Caitlin moved in on him, playing the age-old role of seductive temptress. She had never done anything like this before, had never felt the need to, but the stakes were high.

All was fair in love and war.

Until now, David had always been one step ahead of her, taking the initiative with a boldness that could still leave her breathless. He had the primitive streak of a hunter who didn't accept being thwarted. If one approach didn't work, he used another, and another, until he had what he wanted.

Why shouldn't she be the same? If this was the game he played, she would play it, too.

She slid her fingers out of her hair and dropped her hands on to his shoulders, kneading the tight muscles with varying pressures. 'You need to relax, David,' she said in a low throaty purr.

'I need to go,' he bit out.

She moved her hands to the back of his neck, caressing the sensitive nape as she lifted simmering green eyes to his. 'Not before you kiss me.' She moved up on tiptoe, brushing her breasts against the fine fabric of his shirt.

'What are you trying to do to me?'

'Find reassurance.'

His chin unbent enough for her mouth to reach his. She ran the tip of her tongue lightly between his lips as she pressed closer, arching her back, pushing her stomach into provocative union with his.

She heard his sharp intake of breath, felt the tingling touch of his tongue as it moved in response to hers. His hands closed possessively over the soft mounds of her buttocks, lifting her higher to meet the burgeoning thrust of desire she had stirred.

She invaded his mouth, sweeping his palate with the feverish purpose of increasing his arousal. She rubbed her stomach and thighs against his in wanton incitement, determined on making him burn for her. There was a fire in her belly that demanded total commitment.

An animal growl came from his throat. One hand splayed across her lower back, crushing her softness around the rigid bulge in his trousers. His other hand thrust through her hair, gripped the back of her head, holding it still as he forcefully invaded her mouth, plundering its sweetness with a passion as feverish as her own.

A feeling of triumph tingled through Caitlin's veins. At long last he had forgotten his schedule. 'Take me,' she whispered huskily as his chest heaved for breath. 'Take me, David.'

She dropped a hand to his shirt, her fingers tearing at the buttons. His stomach contracted as he muttered some fierce imprecation. Then suddenly, brutally, his hands were encircling her upper arms, pushing her away from him. It startled her into a cry of protest. Her gaze flew up, wild and accusing and mournful, meeting a blaze of furious blue.

'You take away a man's brain and leave him witless.'

'You want me,' she cried. *As she wanted him*.

'You tempt me beyond endurance.'

'Isn't that what men want from the women they never marry!' she flung back at him.

'I've never referred to or alluded to you in any way to imply that you were my *mistress*.'

'You just have,' she said with infinite regret and a deadness of soul.

'You goaded me into this, Caitlin,' he responded. 'I don't know what the hell you think you're playing at, but this isn't the time for it.'

'When will there be time for it?' she fired at him, seething with frustration, crushed by his remorselessness.

A shutter came down on the blue blaze. '*Maybe never*.'

'That's what I thought,' she said heavily. It justified everything she had said and done. Her voice shook with the vehemence of her feeling of rejection. 'I won't be here tonight.'

If he had ever *liked* her he would have known that already. He would have found out. The truth was that he wasn't interested in what made her tick, what made her the person she was.

His eyes narrowed. He plucked his hands away from her. 'Neither will I,' he snapped, not understanding what was happening but not bending a millimetre.

'Just as you have a life I don't share, I have a life you don't share,' Caitlin threw at him. Her chin tilted defiantly. 'You can take me now or leave me now. If you leave, I don't know when I'll be free again.'

His mouth took on a cynical twist. 'Barter-time, is it?'

Her eyes flashed contempt. 'Sorting out priorities.'

That gave him pause for thought. She could almost see his mind clicking over with calculations. 'We'll talk about this later,' he said, and turned to go.

'Don't worry about turning on the percolator in the kitchen for me. I'll do it myself.'

His eyes turned back to her with a dark, turbulent glare. His trousers still bulged. It had to be causing him some physical distress to leave her like this. His head jerked away.

Caitlin didn't follow him out of the bedroom. She stood precisely where she was until she heard the door to her apartment click shut behind him. He still hadn't asked her what she was doing tonight, why she wouldn't be free for him. He didn't care what she did when she wasn't with him.

She shivered.

It spurred her to a burst of activity. She grabbed a robe from her cupboard and marched out to the kitchen, wrapping herself tightly in the all-enveloping garment. She filled the coffee-maker and switched it on, feeling furiously justified in not having done it for David this morning. He didn't deserve it. He didn't deserve anything from her.

Her eye caught the calendar hanging below the kitchen clock. Today's date was ringed. It was important. February the fourteenth. St Valentine's Day. The day her mother and father were married thirty years ago. The day she was given Dobbin as her very own pony. The day for lovers to declare themselves. A day to concentrate on romance. A day which would be as bleak as Hades because she had danced with the devil.

A wave of nausea cramped Caitlin's stomach and pushed a choking lump into her throat. She tore off the offending page of February and crushed it in her hand. She didn't need the reminder of her parents' wedding anniversary any more, and she certainly didn't need a reminder of what she didn't have with David Hartley.

She opened the lid of the kitchen tidy and threw the crumpled wad of paper into the bin. She wished she could get rid of her unrequited love for David Hartley just as easily.

She looked up at the clock. She had an hour and forty-two minutes to don her role as his personal assistant and wear the label 'For Office Use Only'. That was what David was going to get from her from now on until he decided differently about sex, sensuality and sharing.

CHAPTER TWO

CAITLIN stepped off the bus at Chatswood at five minutes to nine. Normally she would take that amount of time to arrive at the Hartley building. Today she was not eager to get to work.

The morning was fine and sparkling. A continuation of last night's violent thunderstorm with its torrential rain would have been more in keeping with Caitlin's dark misery. The intense blueness of a cloudless sky appeared to mock the bleak prospect of her future.

She had made the effort to present a meticulous appearance. David paid her a large salary. He expected her to perform well and look stylish and sophisticated.

Pride insisted she give him no grounds for any possible criticism where her job was concerned. It also insisted that she show no sign of the deep distress he had given her. As a result she looked particularly bright and shiny, so much so that she attracted a second look from many other pedestrians as she crossed the road to her place of business.

Her hair was freshly washed and blow-dried into a gleaming cascade of waves. It brought out the gold streaks in the darker tawny mass. It also provided a strikingly sensual frame for what was an

essentially feminine face, oval in shape and set on
a long Nefertiti neck. Her eyes were large, deeply
lidded and emphasised with finely arched brows.
Her nose was small and straight, the slight flare of
her nostrils balancing a generous mouth.

Caitlin had applied a soft and subtle make-up;
only a fine touch of shadow and eyeliner to em-
phasise the green of her thickly lashed eyes, a barely
discernible brush of colour to highlight her cheekbones, and a dusting of very expensive powder to
give her skin a smooth lustre. The curves of her
mouth were perfectly outlined with a tan lip-pencil
and filled in with peach gloss.

She wore an elegant long-sleeved blouse in a soft
cream voile with lace inserts running down the
bodice. Her long button-through crêpe skirt was of
a darker cream, slim-lined and fitted snugly to her
small waist. Her stockings were of fine quality, her
court shoes taupe suede to match her shoulder-bag.

She looked a picture of style, which was what
David Hartley expected of her. As Caitlin walked
up the steps to the main entrance of the Hartley
building, the showroom manager hurried forward
to open the door for her, casting an appreciative
eye over her appearance and giving her a wel-
coming smile. 'Good morning, Miss Ross,' he said
cheerfully.

She dredged up a smile. 'Good morning, Mr
Jordan.' He was a slickly handsome man in his early
forties, always a bit too effusive for Caitlin's liking,
but that probably went with being a top salesman.
David did not employ second-rate staff.

He grinned. 'May I wish you a very happy St Valentine's Day. And lots of lovers!'

Caitlin barely stopped herself from wincing. The greeting was undoubtedly meant as today's variation of 'Have a nice day.' Paul Jordan made it sound offensive.

'Thank you,' she said, and hurried past him into the foyer.

She didn't so much as glance at the vast showroom that took up most of the ground floor. It was packed with state-of-the-art office furniture, all designed to accord with David Hartley's specialised standards. These were directly related to his study of the engineering aspects of the relationship between workers and their environment. When it came to ergonomics, no one knew more about it, or had cornered the market more effectively.

Caitlin headed straight for the elevator that would take her to the administrative offices on the first floor. Jenny Ashton, the telephonist and receptionist, looked up from her desk. She was two years younger than Caitlin, a pretty blonde with an infectious smile. The smile broadened to full beam as though she was bursting with good news.

'Hi, Jenny!' Caitlin greeted her briefly and quickened her step. She didn't have the time or the inclination for chat this morning.

'Great day!' Jenny returned, her brown eyes sparkling.

'Sure,' Caitlin agreed. She forced another smile. 'Did your boyfriend give you something special?' she asked in passing, trying to look pleased for her.

Jenny rolled her eyes expressively. 'I'd certainly call it special.'

'Good for you!' Caitlin called back to her as she pressed the elevator button.

The door opened immediately. It was a relief to relax her facial muscles as she stepped into the compartment. Common sense argued that she should break with David right now. He was never going to give her what she wanted. To stay on as his assistant could only be a torment to her. She told herself he had dazzled her into a love-affair. Her eyes were now well and truly open, and she knew where it was all leading to. Nowhere!

The problem was, she was addicted to him. The thought of never again experiencing the wild passion they shared together sent a wave of empty desolation through her body. Nor were there jobs of this quality lurking around every corner. Would she ever get another that would match this one?

David emitted a charge of electricity that made even the most mundane work appear exciting and fulfilling. She felt his intensity and responded to it. Would she ever meet another man to match him?

Was she prepared to end the addiction...cold turkey?

The thought was depressing.

Feeling emotionally torn by the prospect, Caitlin stepped out of the elevator and walked to her office on automatic pilot. She checked her watch as she opened the door. It was precisely nine o'clock. Her timing was perfect, not a minute early, not a minute late.

She sniffed in puzzlement. A sweet, rich scent seemed to permeate the room. She looked up, then stared in astonishment at the magnificent arrangement of red roses sitting on her desk. There had to be dozens of dark velvety buds beginning to unfurl into full bloom. Incredibly beautiful, marvellous, heart-kicking extravagance!

Warmth flooded through her veins. Red roses were for love. Red roses were for eternity.

David must have relented. He had seen the errors of his ways. He didn't want to lose her. Maybe he did love her.

Or perhaps he had ordered the roses yesterday. Which was why he wouldn't consider any change in his schedule today. He knew what was to be delivered this morning. He wanted her to be surprised by his gift of love.

Caitlin moved forward like a sleepwalker. Her mind was abuzz with exciting possibilities. Attached to the decorative basket from which the roses sprayed in luxurious splendour was a large and fabulously elaborate St Valentine's Day card.

A red satin heart was outlined in lace and seed pearls. The card itself had a mother-of-pearl sheen and above the heart was a fat little cupid set in gold, shooting an arrow at a heart. Her heart!

Caitlin's fingers trembled as she opened it. Her pulse raced with the hope that David had written something personal and meaningful, something that might indicate his real commitment to her.

The hope was somewhat deflated. Within a wreath of roses was printed 'Be My Valentine'. No address to her. No signature. Only the single message of the card.

But that was something. It was an advance on what had gone before. A lilt of happiness dispelled the disappointment. It was certainly more than she had ever expected from David. He was not given to sentimentality. He did not celebrate anniversaries.

She grinned as the realisation struck her that Jenny and Mr Jordan had both seen the roses arrive. Jenny had probably shown the delivery person to her office. Did they realise that David would not put his name on the card? Did they even suspect what was going on between them?

He certainly wouldn't hand-write anything on such a public gift. Other employees would see he was flagrantly breaking his own rules. That would not be good for morale. But she knew, and she was the only one who was meant to know. Their love-affair *was* a private thing. She would make certain it was kept that way.

Caitlin breathed in the wonderfully intoxicating scent, then with a happy sigh set about preparing for work. She hung her shoulder-bag on the coat-stand, grabbed her shorthand pad and pen from the top desk drawer, and headed for the door that led into David's office.

It was amazing. Five minutes ago she would have approached this door with every muscle in her body twanging and twitching with tension. Now she was eager to face David again, delighted he had unbent so far for her sake. He understood. He had given her a pleasure that he wouldn't care about for himself. It was a turning point, a concession, a gesture that proved he cared about her feelings.

She opened the door and breezed in, bubbling with new confidence. David's eyes snapped up from the papers on his desk. There was a fractional tightening of his jaw. He had the gritty look of a man who had been placed in the front line of battle, determined not to be seen shirking his duty, but hating the position of vulnerability. His eyes bored into Caitlin; angry, distrustful, broodingly belligerent.

'You're late,' he accused bitingly.

Caitlin barely repressed what was almost an irrepressible smile. Then it burst on to her lips like irradiating sunshine. 'I was thinking of you.'

David looked taken aback by her response. He was uncertain of her. That was the problem. He didn't like being uncertain of her, but he was. She had acted in an unpredictable manner this morning. He wasn't sure which way she would jump now. His applecart had been upset, his sense of purpose and direction severely changed.

To Caitlin this was proof enough that she *was* important to him. She did have some influence over his thinking. This was not the time, however, to break any more of his rules. She was not supposed to be a recipient of roses from him, so it would be unwise to thank him openly for them until they were out of the office and away from work. Nevertheless, she could let him know her feelings without being direct.

'I didn't mean to hold you up, David,' she said in quick apology, 'but you're full of surprises today.' She looked at him meaningfully.

'So, too, are you,' came the somewhat uncertain reply.

She gave him another brilliant smile as she walked briskly forward and sat in the chair she used for taking dictation. Even looking as stern as he did, David was devastatingly handsome. He was wearing a navy-blue suit. It was the fashionable colour in the corporate world. It looked superb on David. A silk tie diagonally striped in red and navy and silvery grey was perfectly aligned on his white shirt. Very impressive. As he always was with business.

'Ready when you are,' she prompted.

He stared at her for ever so long, as though weighing her present mood against the crackling hostility that had burst upon him earlier. He did not relax and smile, but his expression softened.

'The German delegation will be here in less than an hour,' he stated, perhaps as a reminder of how unreasonable she had been in asking him to take the day off.

'I'm sorry about this morning,' she said, letting him know she was in a far more reasonable frame of mind now.

'So am I,' he murmured reasonably, and immediately came back to business. 'The delegation desperately want the licence to manufacture, but they'll try to work the price down by finding faults in our design.'

'I know this deal is important to you,' Caitlin added, reassuring him of her complete co-operation. It made her happy to think he was genuinely sorry for their earlier contretemps.

His brows lowered. His eyes sharply probed hers. 'Are you concentrating on what I'm saying?'

'Every word. All the unsaid ones, too.' She smiled again to show there were absolutely no hard feelings left on her side.

His face took on a wary expression. He rapped out his instructions as though testing her shorthand speed. 'Arrange for Paul Jordan to come in and announce that we have the Sutherland contract. That's to be half an hour after we start. Make sure his timing is perfect. When I want you to come and sit in on the meeting and take notes, I'll buzz you on the phone.'

'Fine,' she said, her pen flashing over her notepad.

He seemed bemused momentarily. 'Is the boardroom fully prepared?'

'I haven't checked it yet. I'll do that immediately.'

Caitlin rose to her feet with crisp efficiency. She was in such buoyant spirits that her walk to the door was unconsciously jaunty.

'Wait!'

She swung around, her eyes brightly expectant. Anything David asked her to do she would carry out to the very best of her ability. She would most certainly be an assistant he would be proud to present in front of the German delegation.

He appeared to be wrestling with some private dilemma. She could feel tension flowing from him, swirling around her. His penetrating blue eyes were intensely concentrated on hers, as though trying to read her mind.

'I want to say...' He paused, cleared his throat. 'How much I appreciate...' Again he stopped, seeming lost for words.

'Understood,' Caitlin responded, realising he was trying to bridge the awkward gap left by their previous parting. 'I do, too.'

'What?'

'Appreciate the...uh...what you're trying to say.'

He weighed that for a moment, then looked relieved. 'Well, as long as everything's working out all right...'

'Yes. I hope it is.' A new dance was definitely in progress, although where it would lead was by no means settled yet.

'Good!' He nodded his approval. The apples were back on his cart.

Caitlin had a moment's disquiet. She recollected his cynical taunt, 'Barter-time, is it?' Were the roses simply a timely gift to keep her sweet? Caitlin didn't like the thought at all. She brushed it aside, not wanting to spoil her pleasure in the gift. Besides, David had returned his attention to the papers on his desk and it behoved her to get about her business immediately.

CHAPTER THREE

CAITLIN set out everything that might be required on the boardroom table, then zipped back to her office to put in a call to Paul Jordan before heading to the kitchen to load up a traymobile with the usual refreshments.

The call to Jordan was deferred by the arrival of a delivery boy with another gift basket for her.

Caitlin was stunned by the contents. Nestled in a froth of red ribbons were a heart-shaped box of hand-made Swiss chocolates, and an enormously expensive set of Beautiful toiletries by Estee Lauder. These included perfume, skin lotion, bath oil and talcum powder. Most amazingly and endearingly of all, there was also a soft toy puppy.

Of all the soft toy animals David might have chosen, that was the second-best. The perfect choice for her would have been a pony, but Caitlin couldn't remember having ever talked about Dobbin to him. Therefore he wouldn't, couldn't, know any better.

Surprises were certainly coming thick and fast this morning! Caitlin's head was spinning with them. It was the way David did things, turning situations around so quickly. He was leaving her breathless and utterly enthralled by what he could do when he set his mind to it.

She suddenly realised time was slipping by. She postponed the call to Paul Jordan and raced to the office kitchen. Coffee, tea, milk, cream, plain and fancy biscuits and mixed sandwiches from catering were mandatory. By five minutes to ten it was all in the boardroom, ready for her to serve when needed. She had barely returned to her office when Jenny called to announce the arrival of the German delegation. Caitlin buzzed David, then went to meet the visitors at reception and escort them to the boardroom.

She carried out her duties with the charm David expected of her. Once everyone was settled around the table, she was free to prime Paul Jordan with what was expected of him. She would drag the Sutherland contract out of the filing system. Paul might as well take that with him.

David smiled at her as she left the boardroom. She hugged the smile to her heart, drifting back to her office on a cloud of happiness.

She couldn't resist dabbing some Beautiful on. It was wonderful perfume, well named. She hadn't been in the mood to bother with perfume this morning. She was now. She hoped David would recognise and appreciate the scent when she sat near him to take notes of the meeting. This was turning out to be a lovely morning, a really *beautiful* morning.

The phone rang just as she reached for it. Caitlin lifted the receiver, intending to take a very quick message so she could call Paul Jordan straight afterwards.

'Caitlin?' Her mother's voice.

'Hi, Mum! Happy wedding anniversary! How's everything going for the party? Anything you need?'

The sound of sobbing. 'Mum, what's wrong?'

More sobbing. 'Mum, please, please, please tell me what's happened.'

'There isn't going to be a party.'

Caitlin was staggered. Her heart sank to the pit of her stomach. 'Why?' she asked, then collected her wits sufficiently to enquire, 'Why not?'

'Your father...' Her mother's voice quavered. She burst into more tears.

Caitlin's worst fears were aroused. Her father had a history of heart disease. 'Tell me the worst,' she said bravely.

'He...he...he...'

'Yes, yes, yes?' Caitlin prompted.

'He walked out on me!'

Caitlin's head spun. This wasn't making sense at all. 'What do you mean—he walked out on you?'

'I mean what I said!' her mother replied, a touch of asperity in her voice. She didn't like to be contradicted or have her communications misunderstood.

Caitlin used her most sympathetic voice. 'He couldn't do that to you.'

'Thirty years of looking after him hand and foot,' her mother wailed. 'I'm disgusted at what he's done. I'll never forgive him. Never! Even if he is your father.'

'There must be a reason,' Caitlin soothed gently. 'Perhaps if I talk to him.'

'You *can't* do that,' her mother snapped peremptorily.

'Why not?'

'I don't know where he's gone to.'

'He can't go too far without money,' Caitlin suggested.

'Oh, he's got money. Too much of it, if you ask me. He's been secretly hoarding everything I gave him without telling me what he was doing.'

'Mum, there has to be a way.'

'Oh, there's a way,' her mother said grimly between sniffles. 'He's done this as a symbol. When I catch up with him, I'll give him a symbol. I'll kill him!'

'Mum, let me think about this.' Caitlin had the feeling that time was passing very rapidly. She still had to get in touch with Paul Jordan. 'Can I get back to you?'

'There's no need, Caitlin. I'm on my own. After thirty years of suffering through your father's moods, this is all the thanks I get. There isn't going to be a wedding anniversary party tonight. There's nothing for you to do. There's nothing anyone can do.'

Caitlin had had no idea that her parents' marriage had been cracking up. On her recent visits home, her father had occasionally been somewhat withdrawn about her mother's current projects and plans, but there had been no indication of a serious falling out. After all the years they had spent together, surely there was some meeting ground left?

'Mum . . . Mum . . .' Caitlin tried to catch her mother's attention.

'Everything's ruined. It'll be the talk of the town!' her mother cried.

And that, Caitlin thought, was probably the crux of the matter. Her mother had always worried too much about what others thought. 'I'll do my best to patch things up,' Caitlin said on a rueful sigh.

'My life is in tatters, Caitlin. Totally and irretrievably ruined.'

Caitlin tried to give a glow of hope. 'Somehow it will turn out right.'

'No, it won't.' Her mother gave another wail of absolute distress and despair, and hung up.

Caitlin ran through a mental list of places where her father might have stormed off to. Before she recollected the important business tactic she had to set in motion, the door to her office opened and in strode David Hartley, emitting enough sparks to start a conflagration.

Caitlin's mind exploded in horror. Time had passed too quickly. It was now too late to call Paul Jordan!

David came to an abrupt halt. He glared at the splendid arrangement of red roses. He glared at the beribboned basket containing the puppy and the chocolates and the luxurious toiletries. His glare swung back to the roses, fastening even more fiercely on the elaborate Valentine Card. Finally, he fired bolts of blue fire straight at Caitlin.

'What the hell is going on out here?'

Caitlin started guiltily from her chair. 'Nothing.'

'Well, something has been going on in there.' David pointed to the boardroom. 'The delegation is not only muttering about alleged design flaws, they've been talking to Crawley.'

Michael Crawley was David's main rival. The mere mention of his name was enough to set David aflame. There was litigation pending between the two companies over patent infringements.

'I'm sorry...'

'I've been trying to contact you for the last twenty minutes,' he grated. 'Your line has been tied up. You've made me look like a first-class idiot.'

She flushed. 'My mother called.'

He looked at her incredulously. 'Where's Jordan?'

Caitlin tried to think of an appropriate reply.

His gaze flashed savagely to the roses, then back to her fiery cheeks. 'Did your mother send the roses?'

'No. You did,' she reminded him.

He looked at her as though she had gone stark raving mad. 'I did no such thing. What do you mean...I gave them to you?'

A great bottomless pit formed in Caitlin's stomach. She wanted the ground to open up and swallow her. She fought down the feeling of emotional panic. 'If you didn't send them, who did?'

'Ask your mother.' His voice dripped acid. His eyes raked hers with scathing disbelief at her dereliction of duty. 'In the meantime, can we get back to running this business?'

Her chin came up in fighting mode. Everything had to be done to the beat of his drum. He didn't listen to her. He didn't understand that she had problems as well as he. He didn't give her roses or consideration or caring. She had duped herself into thinking David had relented in his tyrannical attitude towards her. He had not bent one iota.

'David, I think we're finished,' she said tightly.

'Damned right!' he agreed. 'Get Jordan up here. He might do the job required of him.'

A stinging rebuff.

She watched him as though from a far distance as he swung on his heel and headed back to the boardroom.

Cold, hard and ruthless. As his competitors saw him. As Michael Crawley must see him. As the German delegation must see him. As Caitlin now saw him.

With a heavy hand, she lifted up the phone. There was no answer from Jordan's office. She rang Jenny.

'Where's Paul Jordan?' she asked bleakly.

'He stepped out for half an hour. Call that the rest of the morning. He thinks he's got a potential deal with the Kirrawee Business College.'

Caitlin's hand was even heavier as she replaced the phone. She had done a thoroughly comprehensive job in stuffing up both her personal life and professional life.

She couldn't rescue the former. That required the impossible to happen. As for the latter, there was only one thing left to do. She went to the filing cabinet and dragged out the Sutherland contract.

She would give the presentation herself.

Not Jordan's way.

Not David's way.

Her way.

CHAPTER FOUR

DAVID, of course, sat at the head of the table in the boardroom. The four men from Germany were spread on either side of him, two on his right, two on his left. Herr Schmidt, the leader of the delegation, was pointing out something in the documents in front of him when Caitlin entered. The attention of the five men swung to her.

David glowered at her. Herr Schmidt frowned at the interruption. The expressions on the other men's faces ranged from interested spectator to a deadpan weighing of what her unheralded appearance meant. They all looked tough, experienced, executive businessmen. None had the magnetic charisma that David could exude so effortlessly.

To Caitlin he dominated the room, just as he had dominated her life for the last four months. The thought spurred her to renewed determination.

No more domination.

This was her swan-song. She would use David's tactics and give them her own twist. She might not be special to him, but he wouldn't forget her in a hurry. Not for what she was about to do. She hoped it would make him burn. In the right places.

She walked briskly to the end of the table, facing David down the length of it. 'Mr Hartley, we have chaos in the office,' she announced, showing no

40

perturbation at all at dropping bombshells in the boardroom.

'*I know that.*' His voice had the low rumble of an incipient earthquake.

'You'll be pleased to hear that the Sutherland contract has arrived. All signed, sealed and delivered,' she stated wearily, as though it was one more chore to deal with on top of everything else.

'Good.' He gave her a frozen smile.

'How we're going to get that amount of product out on to the market in time, I do not know.'

'Miss Ross...' he looked sharply at the German delegation '...please take control of yourself.'

'Fifteen hundred units,' she burbled on. He knew as well as she knew how *grossly exaggerated* that figure was. The German delegation did not.

'Miss Ross,' he said sharply, 'this is confidential information. Please be careful what you say. Where's Jordan?'

She aimed a sigh of exasperation at him. 'Mr Jordan left to clinch a huge deal with a string of business colleges,' she went on, treating his warning about confidentiality as totally irrelevant in the circumstances. 'Sell, sell, sell. That's all he can do. The man is like a robot.'

'I didn't know he'd gone.' David looked vexed. 'He's supposed to be here.'

'I haven't had a moment to tell you.' Caitlin put some vexation into her voice. 'As you're aware, the phone-lines have been engaged all morning. All the other salesmen are out, too. Every blasted one of them. We can't cover the volume of work that's pouring in. For one thing, we need more phone-lines ...'

David passed a weary hand over his face. 'What point are you coming to, Miss Ross?'

'There's an overload of work. I'm needed else-where. The matter is urgent,' she stated emphati-cally. 'I require permission to leave the office. It's mandatory. I need to take the afternoon off to attend to what has to be done.'

Danger signals glimmered in his eyes. 'I have guests here from a foreign country who have to be attended to and looked after with the proper courtesy and respect, Miss Ross. Permission refused!'

Caitlin set her mouth into a long-suffering line. She threw a glance at the heavens as though praying for patience. She had seen him do the same action this morning, so had no trouble in duplicating it. It didn't work any better for her than it did for him.

Patience was not bestowed on her.

She dropped her gaze to David and gave him a long, glittering glare. Then she tossed her hair in defiance, flounced around the table to where he sat, and slapped the Sutherland file down in front of him.

'Sir!' She took a deep breath. Her breasts lifted, drawing every eye on either side of the table to the lace inserts of her blouse. Her hands planted them-selves on her hips. 'Something has to give,' she de-clared with passionate conviction. 'It's prob-ably me!'

Everyone was quite fascinated by now. She had their full attention. Including David's. Especially David's. She hoped he was getting the underlying personal message loud and clear. She was not going to go his way any more.

'Something *is* going to give,' he said grimly, 'and I agree that it's likely to be you.'

'You need to employ more staff.'

'I'll certainly be dealing with that, Miss Ross.' The purpose behind those words was unmistakable. She had not only crossed the Rubicon, she had committed hara-kiri on every level by not staying in the pigeonhole he'd built for her.

'Can we go into recess on this?' She would give him one last chance to be reasonable.

'Not at the present moment.'

Green eyes sizzled into blue, giving him her message in no uncertain terms. 'Very well,' she snapped. 'Please understand I can no longer handle all you require of me. I cannot meet the standards you demand of me. The overtime is excessive and unrewarding. We have come to the end of the line, you and I. *Finis*. Full stop. Goodbye.'

He was rising to his feet. 'Miss Ross!' he cried out hoarsely, obviously shaken to his bootstraps. Such antics had never been seen in this boardroom before.

'Stay where you are, Mr Hartley. There's no need to say or do anything. Business comes first. Remember this morning.' She hoped he did.

With another toss of her hair she turned to march away from him. There was one last thing she could

do. She would do it and end this farce. She took
three steps, stopped, then swung back to address
the head of the German delegation. Herr Schmidt
was a big, burly man with sharp grey eyes. He had
a poker face, revealing nothing of his thoughts.

'There are no design defects in our products, Herr
Schmidt. You are wasting our time. Mr Hartley is
simply being too polite to tell you that to your face.'

The implication was clear. If he chose not to buy
the licence, the loss was his, not theirs. She gave
him a full eyeful of scorn, then resumed her march
from the room, her hair swinging, her hips
swinging, and the deal with the German delegation
swinging.

Five pairs of eyes followed her out of the room.
No one broke the silence which enveloped them.

Win or lose, Caitlin didn't care any more. If
David didn't want to play the hand she had dealt
him, that was too bad! As best she could, she had
made up for her lapse in carrying out his instructions. The dance with the devil was over. She closed
the door behind her with finality.

That action did nothing to fill the aching void in
her heart. Why do women love so foolishly? she
wondered. They hurt only themselves.

Back in her own office, the strong scent of the
roses mocked the secret dreams and desires she had
so fondly nurtured. The irrational hope she had so
blindly fostered in her heart was dead. David
Hartley was never going to change. The romance
in his soul was encased in concrete surrounded by
barbed wire and porcupine quills.

But it was best not to think about him now. She had to act on the decision she had made. No wavering. No waiting. There would be no softening coming from him. If she took nothing else away from her association with David Hartley, she would take her self-esteem and self-respect.

Tears pricked her eyes as she walked around her desk and flopped listlessly into her chair. She had been so happy to receive such lovely gifts. Why couldn't it have been David asking her to 'be his Valentine'? She had no idea who else might be declaring his interest in her. She wasn't interested in anyone else. Someone had wasted an awful lot of money on nothing.

Maybe it was a mistake. Perhaps the Valentine gifts were meant for someone else. A mistake could easily be made because there was no name on the card. She was probably the recipient of mischance and some other woman was missing out on the pleasure meant for her.

With a heavy sigh, Caitlin rolled her chair around to face her computer. She switched it on and brought up the Microsoft Word program. It wouldn't take long to type up an official letter of resignation to end her employment by David Hartley. She would leave it on his desk and go.

Her mother needed her. Her father had to be found. As far as her family was concerned, this St Valentine's Day had brought nothing but misery and despair. Caitlin hoped she could do more for her parents than she could do for herself. Her one-sided love-affair was definitely on skid-row, but if her parents' marriage could be rescued, at least that would be something.

Her fingers flew over the keyboard. She re-read what she had typed on to the monitor, nodded her satisfaction, then switched on the laser printer and waited for the fateful page to roll out.

She was on her feet, ready to pick up the page and sign her name to it, when she heard her office door open. She glanced around automatically.

Her heart thudded with apprehension when she saw David enter and close the door behind him. She didn't want another confrontation with him. What was over was over.

'Caitlin...'

'You're supposed to be looking after your guests.'

The printer whirred. She turned back to it. David could say what he liked. She wasn't going to let it affect her. The page that would put an end to everything between them rolled towards her.

'We've gone into recess for twenty minutes to re-establish contact with reality,' he stated, conveniently forgetting that he had ruled out a recess when *she* had suggested it. 'We're going to relook at what direction we're all coming from,' he went on, his voice coming closer and closer. He paused. 'Caitlin, you were *magnificent*!'

An accolade indeed, coming from David, but it came too late. Caitlin steeled her heart against responding to him.

The phone rang.

David automatically picked it up. Slowly and deliberately, Caitlin signed her resignation.

'It's for you,' he said, holding the receiver out to her.

She put down the pen, picked up the page and walked back to her desk. He stood on the other side of it, waiting for her. His face carried an interrogation mark. He looked puzzled. He frowned at the roses and expensive toiletries.

Caitlin took the phone and handed him the page containing her resignation. He didn't lower his gaze to read it. His eyes quizzed hers, trying to understand what was going on. She ignored him.

'Caitlin Ross speaking.'

'Caitlin, this is your father.'

Her attention was immediately arrested. Her father sounded distressed. Her heart went out to him. What misery could he have endured to make him snap at such a time, on the very day he should have been celebrating thirty years of marriage with the woman he had once loved?

'Oh, Dad...' She didn't know what else to say. Somehow those two words summed up her feelings.

'I'm sorry, Caitlin. I have bad news for you.'

'Tell me about it,' she said gently. She had to listen to both sides, act as the peace-maker, help find a reconciliation between them if one could be found.

'It's Dobbin, Caitlin. He's been terribly, severely injured.'

'Oh, no!' A wail of deep distress. Her pony. Her friend and confidante since she was eleven years old. In many ways that horse had filled gaps in her life more than any human being. 'How?' she cried. 'What happened?'

A defeated sigh. 'He panicked during the thunderstorm last night. He became entangled in a barbed wire fence.'

Her heart contracted painfully. Barbed wire could rip a horse to shreds. A tremor of premonition ran through her, making her feel weak and shaky. She reached for her chair, pulled it towards her, sat down. 'Is he...?' She had to know. But she couldn't quite bring herself to face the worst. 'How...how badly is he torn?'

'I'm sorry, Caitlin.' Her father's voice was sad and wistful. He knew how much the old pony meant to her. 'We couldn't let him suffer. We had to put him down.'

She could not strangle the wail of protest at the futilities of life. It welled from deep inside her and found utterance on her lips. Her chest heaved once, twice, three times. The burgeoning grief could not be suppressed. It was too much to bear...the death of her hopes for David's love, the death of her parents' marriage, and now the very real death of her beloved old pony. She hadn't even been there to nurse his head, stroke him once more, say goodbye...

Tears formed in large droplets and gathered pace as they streamed down her cheeks. She slumped forward, propped her elbow on the desk, and covered her face with her hand as she wept.

This had to be the most wretched day of her life.

'Caitlin?' Her father's voice, pained and anxious.

'Caitlin?' David's voice, oddly strained for him.

She struggled to regain control of herself, control of the situation. There were things she had to do. 'Dad, where are you?' she choked out. 'I need...to see you...talk to you.'

She dropped her hand, her fingers scrambling blindly for a pen to write down whatever address he gave her. David's gold pen was pressed into her hand, a notepad placed in front of her.

'I'm at a pub. Don't feel like going home, Caitlin,' her father said flatly.

'What pub, Dad?'

'The Last Retreat. It's down the Yarramalong Road.'

It took Caitlin three attempts before she had it correctly written down. Slowly she replaced the phone, set the pen aside, peeled off the note page, pushed herself to her feet and set a course for the coatstand where she'd hung her shoulder-bag.

She was waylaid by a broad chest and arms that gently cradled her against it. 'What's happened, Caitlin?'

She stared at David's throat. She had never heard it produce words that sounded more sympathetic and sincere. Once she had craved for them. Even now, she had a craven wish to lean on the warmth and strength his body seemed to promise. She needed loving very badly. But David Hartley wouldn't give that to her. Not the kind of loving she needed. It seemed almost funny that her tears had moved him as nothing else had. Maybe she should have wept more often.

'Let me go, David,' she demanded tonelessly.

'Caitlin, let me help you,' he said earnestly. 'Tell me what's wrong. If there's something I can do to help, let me do it.'

'It's too late for that, David.'

'It's never too late.'

He was wrong. No one could turn back the clock and save Dobbin. He would probably think her a sentimental fool for grieving over an old pony. Sentiment was not David's strength. Caitlin had had ample proof of that.

'You've never cared about my feelings for you or for my family. Never bothered asking about them. You didn't let any thought of my needs infringe on your personal life,' she stated as a matter of incontrovertible fact.

'I didn't realise . . .'

'You only had two concerns,' she went on, relentless in her indictment of his self-centredness. 'Business and sex. I'm not sure even now which came first on your list of priorities, but I tend to think it was business.'

'I care about you, Caitlin,' he said stiffly. 'I care a lot.'

'No . . . no . . .' The pained truth of his feelings for her was reflected in her eyes as she dragged her gaze up to his. 'Not enough. You only care about me when it suits your convenience, David. I'm nothing more than that. You use me to serve your needs.'

An angry flush—or was it one of guilt?—speared across his cheekbones. 'That's not true. You're more important to me than . . .' He hesitated.

'Your precious schedule!' she finished for him.

The flush deepened on his cheekbones. She had hit him hard and low with something he could not deny.

'There's reason enough for that,' he snapped.

'I'm sure there is. You have a reason for everything.'

'So do you.'

She pushed out of his embrace, grabbed her bag from the coatstand and slung it over her shoulder. 'I'm going now,' she said with unshakeable determination.

'You're really resigning!' He sounded bewildered.

'Darned right I am.'

He thrust his hands out in appeal. 'Tell me why!'

'Because you're a heartless, insensitive, callous brute,' she hurled at him.

It smacked home, too. He flinched. 'I know you're upset, Caitlin,' he retorted imperiously. 'You're in a temper. If you want compassionate leave, take it.'

'No need,' she said tightly. 'I'm not coming back.'

'Let's have a cooling-off period.'

She looked her disdain for that idea. 'I'm already cold where you're concerned, David.'

'Tell me what I can do,' he demanded, still sure he had the power to sway her.

'I don't want to. If I told you, you'd only reject it. Just as you reject almost everything about me. Just as you rejected me this morning.'

'I had the Germans coming!' he cried in exasperation.

'You made your choice!' she snapped. 'That's your bed. Lie in it. You can go back to your German delegation now.'

She stepped around him and headed for the door.

'It's not what I want.'

'You should have thought of that earlier.'

'Caitlin!'

She ignored the hoarse command and kept going, opening the door without a backward glance. Before she could close it, he was beside her. She walked on towards the elevator. David matched her step.

'What do you want from me?' he grated out, frustration underscoring every word.

'Nothing.'

'You're the best assistant I've ever had.'

'Thank you.'

'I can't do without you.'

'Tough.'

'I'll raise your salary.'

'I can't be bought.'

'I'll improve your conditions.'

'Too late.'

'Isn't there anything I can do to change your mind?'

'No.'

'What the hell am I going to do?'

'Stick to business, David. You're better at that than human relationships.'

She reached the elevator and pressed the 'down' button. 'I'm going to miss you,' he said.

Caitlin said nothing. She was going to miss him too, but there was no way she could tell him that.

'Who gave you the roses and the other fripperies?'

The elevator door opened. She stepped into the compartment, pressed the button for the ground floor and turned to look at the man she had loved. His face was a study of conflicting and violent emotions.

'I don't know who gave me the St Valentine gifts,' she said sadly, 'but it should have been you, David. It should have been you.'

The door slid between them and closed.

CHAPTER FIVE

CAITLIN was surviving on nervous energy. Inwardly she felt pummelled, stricken, destroyed and destitute.

She took a taxi from the Hartley building to her apartment where she quickly discarded her office clothes. What was needed for David was far too fancy for her father. In his opinion, fashion was a lot of silly nonsense. Very down-to-earth was her dad.

She pulled on a T-shirt, a pair of jeans and her old battered Reeboks, then raced to the bathroom to clean off what was left of her tear-riddled make-up. The mirror revealed she didn't look all that good. Certainly not at the top of her form. It would have to do.

She grabbed what she needed in the way of toiletries, and headed back to the bedroom to pack enough clothes to see her through a week. She didn't know if her parents would get back together again, but she might end up staying with her father, staying with her mother, or jockeying between the two of them until something was straightened out.

She had little doubt that her older sister would stand staunchly by her mother. Michelle had always been Mummy's little girl, while Caitlin, six years her junior, was very much her father's daughter. If any rapprochement could be made, Caitlin knew she was the most likely catalyst.

She hastily swapped the essentials from her suede shoulder-bag to the leather one she favoured for practical purposes, collected her suitcase, locked her apartment, and headed for her car.

Caitlin loved her little car. The Mazda 121 was cute and friendly with its rounded curves. David had laughingly called it a cartoon bubble car, but Caitlin had not let his amusement spoil her pleasure in it. She didn't care about flash performance or a status statement. It was the first car she could call her very own and she loved it.

As she walked along the parking bays of the carport attached to the block of apartments, it occurred to her that throwing in her job with David could change her financial position quite drastically. On the basis of the salary David had paid her, she had moved from a shared apartment to having the luxury of a one-bedroom apartment to herself. She had taken on the commitment of paying for a car. If she didn't land some comparable job very quickly, she would have to shed either the car or the apartment.

The future took on a bleaker prospect.

Caitlin fought off the threatening wave of overwhelming depression. She had made the right decision in parting from David. She would not sell her soul for money. If the car had to go, it would be a far less heart-wrenching loss than Dobbin.

As for the apartment, she had shared one before and she could share again. That was no great hardship. She had enough grief to deal with at the present moment. She would worry about tomorrow when tomorrow came.

She didn't actually *need* a car. She still caught the bus to and from work rather than fight peak-hour traffic for such a short trip. She used it more for weekend travelling than anything else. For the situation Caitlin found herself in today, her little car was invaluable. She settled herself into it with a sense of relief and comfort, and started the journey north.

She thought over her parents' lives as she drove out of Sydney and along the Newcastle expressway. Everything had changed quite dramatically for them two years ago. An estate developer had offered a huge amount of money for their farm at Mardi, an irresistible sum of money to her mother's mind. She had nagged her husband into selling, much against his personal inclinations.

They now had a lovely brick home in the nearby township of Wyong, in the same street where Michelle lived with her husband and three young children. It was precisely where her mother wanted to be. Caitlin was aware that her father was not quite so happy with it.

He missed the farm. He didn't know what to do with himself. He was bored silly. Planning the next trip to some distant part of the world he hadn't seen and didn't wish to see was not his idea of having a purpose in life. His most prized Galloway horses and Caitlin's pony had been agisted on a property at Wyong Creek. Keeping an eye on them was his only link to all he had given up.

Caitlin's mother considered that quite enough. They had earned their retirement and now was the time to enjoy it before they became too old. It had seemed a valid argument. Yet for some reason, which had to be very cogent to him, her father had walked out on her mother. Today of all days!

Caitlin left the expressway at the Wyong exit and took the route through Mardi to link up with the road to Yarramalong. She felt a twinge of sadness as she passed the old farm, now subdivided into two-and-a-half-acre housing lots. She had spent a very happy childhood on that land.

Life is change, she told herself, but some changes cut very deeply at fundamental values.

She wondered how much David would miss her. Would he miss her at all? She berated herself for the speculation. It was futile. To David, whose life centred on his needs, she was already yesterday's woman. He would have a replacement lined up before he left the office today.

She had to shut him out of her mind. And heart.

A roadside sign gave the distance to 'The Last Retreat' as two kilometres. Caitlin knew it was more a country lodge than a pub. The signboard outside the main building listed horseriding among the activities available for guests.

As she parked her car in the area set aside for visitors, she saw her father's pick-up truck outside one of the motel-style units. She decided to bypass the reception desk inside the lodge and go directly to the unit her father was undoubtedly occupying.

It was one-thirty. Time was of the essence. If there was to be an anniversary party tonight, it was due to start at seven-thirty. If it hadn't been already cancelled.

She knocked on the door long and hard before it was opened. Her father looked terrible; unshaven, his clothes crumpled, and worst of all, with an air of defeat written all over him.

Caitlin went straight into his arms, hugging him with a fierce love that wanted to make everything better for him, yet ending up blubbering on his shoulder.

He patted her back and stroked her hair, still his little girl despite the passage of years that had turned her into a young woman. 'There, there,' he soothed. 'Everything is all right.'

'I wish it were.'

'It's for the best. Take my word on it.'

'I'm trying to, Dad,' she sniffed.

'What happened to Dobbin wouldn't have happened if we'd still had the farm. I'd have gone out to have a look at him.'

'It's not your fault, Dad.'

'I don't know, Caitlin. I should never have agreed to what your mother wanted. We've never had a happy day since.'

Caitlin took a deep breath. This was the problem that had to be faced without any further delay. She looked up pleadingly. 'Dad, you and Mum have now got all the things most people dream about.

You worked hard, battled hard, struggled hard. You should be able to enjoy the good things in life.'

'We sold out for money,' he said heavily, 'and they spoiled it. Some of the best grazing land in these parts. I knew every inch of it, every blade of grass.'

'You don't want to let go, do you, Dad?'

'No, Caitlin, I don't want to let go.'

He stroked her cheek in rueful tenderness, smudging away the tears. 'You're a good girl, Caitlin. The one bright spot in my life.'

She choked on another well of emotion. But she could not allow herself to be diverted. She swallowed hard and cut straight to the crisis that had to be tackled.

'Mum rang me, Dad.'

He grimaced and turned away. 'I suppose you got an earful.'

'She was upset.'

He sat on the side of the bed, elbows on his knees, head down, a picture of dejection. 'I didn't want to go home after we'd put Dobbin down, Caitlin. Your mother wants everything her way. Won't listen to anything else. Doesn't care what I feel!'

Caitlin felt a strong sense of empathy with her father. It was precisely what David Hartley had made her feel. Only *his* needs were important.

She sat down on a chair close to him and stroked his arm. 'Tell me about it, Dad,' she invited sympathetically.

He shook his head but the words spilled out. 'She nags and nags...' Her father's list of grievances ran a mile long but essentially they came back to one thing. He was bored out of his mind. He didn't fit into the kind of life her mother was set on leading. 'So I rang her from here,' he concluded, 'and told her the good or bad news, as the case may be.'

'It's bad news,' Caitlin assured him. 'Mum couldn't stop crying on the phone.'

Her father's face set in stubborn lines. 'She'll get over it soon enough. I'm only a nuisance to her. I'm in the way.'

Caitlin didn't plead her mother's case. Her father was in no mood to hear it. For all she knew, the marriage might have reached irretrievable breakdown, and she had no solution to the problem. However, it seemed to her that after thirty years there should be some foundation left for her parents to talk over their differences and come to a better understanding.

Providing, of course, that the party went ahead tonight.

That was critical. If her father refused to budge, and her mother felt humiliated in front of all her friends and acquaintances, the unforgivable would have been committed.

'What do you want, Dad?'

'The way it was. I would go up the street without twenty cents in my pocket and get anything I wanted. Then your mother would go and pay for it next week. I'll say that for your mother. She could manage money. She never, in all our lives, spent more than I earned.'

'Why can't you do that now?' Caitlin asked with some perplexity.

'No one knows anyone any more. It's all shopping malls, and no one's got time to talk to you, and your mother wants to impress people with what we've got. I say we haven't got anything. Lost the lot.'

'We can't put the clock back, Dad. Change is inevitable. We all have to adapt. You. Me. Mum. All of us.'

'Your mother's taken one path. I've taken another. In the diamond of life, our routes have diverged.'

Caitlin knew her rescue mission was in deep trouble. When her father started applying his 'diamond of life' philosophy to his own marriage, divorce was definitely on his mind.

For years now he had been shaking his head over the increasing divorce-rate, particularly among the younger generation. He likened the bottom point of the diamond to the day of the marriage. The lines leading outwards from that point represented the growing apart process that had to be stopped and turned upwards to a point of togetherness again. Young people, he had declared, weren't prepared to work at turning the corner.

Maybe some corners were unturnable, Caitlin had argued.

From the set look of resignation on her father's face, Caitlin had little doubt he was applying her argument to his situation.

There was a knock on the door. Probably someone from the housekeeping staff, Caitlin thought, and was relieved when her father got up to answer it. She had to do some fast thinking, approach the problem from a different angle. That was what David always did when he ran into a brick wall. It usually worked for him.

Perhaps if she pointed out the possibility of the division of family loyalties, it might give her father pause for reconsideration. He did love Michelle and his grandchildren. He might not have thought of consequences like that. There was so much to be weighed in the balance before diving off the deep end.

Caitlin recollected that she hadn't exactly done a profit and loss sheet before parting from David this morning. But that was a serious matter of personal priorities, she firmly assured herself, with no family involved. Besides, four months hardly measured up against thirty years.

She was vaguely aware of the door being opened. She glanced at her watch. Two-thirty. By three o'clock she would need some grounds for a truce if she was to talk her mother around in time to save tonight's party.

'Mr Ross?'

Caitlin's heart stopped dead. There was no mistaking that voice... the deep, penetrating timbre, the confident authority in it. But what was the owner of the voice doing outside her father's room at The Last Retreat?

'Yes,' her father responded automatically.

'I'm David Hartley...'

No possible mistake!

'...Caitlin's employer.'

Caitlin clenched her teeth. *Not any more!*

'Ex-employer,' he self-corrected.

Exactly!

'And friend.'

Since when?

'Caitlin is very deeply distressed.'

With good reason!

'I wish to do everything I can do to sort the problem out!'

As a statement of intention, it sounded good. Her father would probably be taken in by it.

'That's very good of you, Mr Hartley.'

Her father *was* taken in by it.

Caitlin wasn't.

She started to burn. There could be only one reason David Hartley was here. He wanted to get his own way, and he would leave her quite breathless with the sheer pace and audacity with which he attacked.

CHAPTER SIX

CAITLIN'S mind whirled. What had happened to the German delegation? Why had David rushed after her like this? He couldn't be burning up all that badly. There was more to this than met the eye. She tried to think of some plan of action which would put David firmly in the place where he belonged. In hell!

'I'm sorry I'm causing so much commotion, Mr Hartley,' her father was saying. 'I was simply doing what I thought best.'

Caitlin's mind whirled again. Her father had no idea what David was talking about and had jumped to the wrong conclusion. Similarly, David had no idea what her father was talking about. Therefore, to Caitlin's way of thinking, the situation could only get worse.

'We need to get together,' David asserted vigorously. 'Get our synchronisation right. Going separate paths leads to nowhere. Or worse.'

'It's good of you to come all this way to tell me that,' her father responded, 'but I'm not sure I agree.'

'Mr Ross, there are times in every man's life when he is not on the same wavelength as his ... er ... partner. Both are not in step to the same tune. When this happens, we have to find the underlying cause and get solutions. I want a solution. Right now.'

Spoken with forceful resolution and followed by silence. Her father was undoubtedly impressed. It wasn't surprising. David was impressive when he unleashed the dynamo of his personality. The fact that he and her father were talking about two entirely different things left something to be desired as far as mutual understanding went.

'I don't know, I'm sure,' her father said, uncertainly. 'I'll see what Caitlin says.'

'She's here, isn't she?'

'Oh, yes, she's here.'

'May I speak with her, please?'

'Not before I do.' Her father turned toward her. 'Caitlin, your Mr Hartley has come all the way from Sydney to tell me I should go back home. What do you think?'

Caitlin wished she could toss David Hartley to the furthermost reaches of the world. She didn't want to see him again. Yet for some extraordinary reason he appeared to be having more effect on her father than she had managed so far. It would be stupid of her to look a gift horse in the mouth at this juncture. She rose to her feet to add her weight to David's opinion.

'I think he could be right, Dad. There has to be a better solution than this.'

'Your mother has certainly been a wonderful woman,' her father mused, 'except when she's in a temper.'

Caitlin had never seen her father in such a state of nervous vacillation in his life. She knew he hated heated arguments. Did anything to avoid them. When he was forced to endure them, he did so in stoic silence. He never raised his voice to anyone. Quite clearly the prospect of facing her mother, who was bound to give him a terrible tongue-lashing, had little appeal.

'Maybe I should go home,' he said, wavering over the idea.

'Would you like me to talk to Mum first?' Caitlin suggested. 'Smooth things over. After all, she won't want to cancel the party.'

Caitlin crossed her fingers behind her back, desperately hoping the party wasn't already cancelled.

Her father's face reflected quiet rebellion. 'I'm not going to say I'm sorry!'

'I don't have the same reluctance,' David said. 'I want to tell Caitlin I'm sorry for everything that's happened.'

Caitlin couldn't hold back her surprise. She wasn't at all confident how sincere David was, but it was the first time he had ever so much as inferred that he could be fallible. 'David...' His name tripped off her tongue, directly acknowledging his presence for the first time.

'It's not your fault,' her father told him, somewhat surprised.

'Wouldn't you agree we need to get together?' David asked, equally surprised.

Caitlin was astounded. Had she somehow jolted David into a reappraisal of himself and his attitudes? Not only had he dropped his precious business to follow her, he was now proposing to get thoroughly mixed up with her family.

On the other hand, he had no idea of what was really happening, so the proposed need for togetherness could be the product of a very confused mind.

'That could be very noisy,' her father warned, 'and messy. I like Caitlin's idea better. Her mother might listen to what she says. Settle down a bit.'

'I'll go with Caitlin,' David said decisively. 'That will give us time to talk over the essentials. Form a new deal. Whatever support Caitlin needs, I'll be at her side.'

Caitlin almost choked. David might not have fully grasped what was going on, but he was seizing an advantage for himself with his usual breathtaking speed.

'Decent of you,' her father said reflectively. He eyed David up and down. 'I'm glad my daughter works for you, Mr Hartley.'

'Dad, I don't work for him any longer,' Caitlin was driven to protest. 'In fact I don't like him one little . . .'

'Caitlin and I have had a little misunderstanding,' David cut in. 'It's all my fault. I intend to change some of my ways, adopt new attitudes.'

'Well, I'll be blowed,' her father remarked.

'It's too late,' Caitlin cried. 'I don't believe him!' she added wildly, but it was a tantalising thought, a seductive thought. She found herself weakening fast.

'Well, you'll have time to talk on your way in to Wyong,' her father said obligingly to David, then turned back to Caitlin. 'I'll wait here until you let me know how your mother feels. That's pretty crucial!'

Caitlin reined in the spate of turbulent emotion. Why confuse the issue for her father? If David was playing games, she might as well stay on the team, at least until she had reached *her* goal.

'I'll see you later, Dad,' she said, moving forward to press a kiss on her father's cheek.

She gave David a don't-touch-me glare as she stepped outside the room. He fell into step beside her as the door of the unit clicked shut behind them.

'What happened to the Germans?' she asked, keeping her gaze trained on the car park. David's eyes could be dynamite when he wanted her.

'I used the same pretext you did. Sales, sales, sales. I told them I was too busy to deal with them today and to get back to me if and when they made up their minds.'

'How did you know where to come?'

'I saw you write down the address.'

Caitlin felt hopelessly mashed up inside. If she was only a convenience to him, why had he put himself out to follow her? Or was he simply prepared to put in some effort to save himself the inconvenience of finding another convenience?

'What is this supposed to mean?' she demanded.

'It means that when you walked out of the office, Caitlin,' he answered quietly, 'I went cold all over!'

He hadn't been burning for her at all. She'd got that wrong. Somehow she felt she was between the devil and the deep blue sea. Then she remembered she didn't have time for either dancing or swimming in uncharted waters.

'Did you really mean what you said to my father? About standing by me and giving me your support?'

'It's obvious you're in the midst of some family crisis. I'll help in any way I can.'

He had helped with her father, unwittingly perhaps, but it had been very timely. He could be of assistance in bringing her mother around to wanting the party more than she wanted to kill her husband. David, in this situation, was a wild card. The unexpected might bring forth responses that could not be drawn by more conventional means.

'I'm not promising anything in return, David.' She glared a sharp warning at him. 'Particularly sex.'

'The thought never crossed my mind.'

'Liar!'

'When it did cross my mind, I instantly discarded it.'

'Why?'

'I felt it was unworthy of you. There's more to you than sex!'

Caitlin wanted a lot of reassurance on that point. 'Give me a list, David,' she demanded sceptically. 'A long list.'

'I can do it. If you come back to work for me, I'll put it on the dictaphone and you can type it up. A really long list.'

The carrot, she thought. He'd probably make it all up between now and then. 'No,' she said firmly. She had been easy for him once. She wasn't going to be easy for him again.

'Give me a chance.'

'You had a chance this morning. A number of them.'

'Caitlin, I did have other things on my mind.'

'So I noticed, David.'

'I'll make it up to you.'

'How?'

'Tomorrow I intend to take you with me and buy your St Valentine's Day gift.'

'In case it's escaped your notice, David, it's St Valentine's Day today.'

'I always intended to do it. After we'd finished with the German delegation,' he hastily added.

And pigs might fly! 'What did you intend to buy me?' she enquired sweetly.

'Whatever you wanted.'

She was right. He didn't have an answer. 'You're inventing this as you go along, David.'

'What do you want most in the world at the present moment, Caitlin?'

'A horse!' The words flew out of her mouth before she had time to think.

'You'd rather have a horse than me?'

'More rewarding,' she asserted.

'Fine. A horse it will be.'

'No, it won't.'

'Why not?'

'Because the first thing you'll want to do after we buy a horse is jump into bed.'

'No, I won't.'

She had to acknowledge he was working harder to get her back than she had ever imagined he would. It gave her pause for thought. 'David, how long can you go without sex?' she asked him seriously.

'A fair while.'

'A year.'

'Caitlin, a year is a very, very, very, very, very long time.' His face depicted horror.

'Six months?'

He looked dazed.

'One month?'

'I would try,' he said dubiously.

'A week?'

'I think I could handle a week. Exercising grim discipline and absolute control, I feel that a week is probably not beyond my capacity.'

Caitlin wondered how much she could alter David's thinking in a week. It could be a measure of how important, how special she was to him, how much he wanted *her*. Not sex. David was the kind of man who could get sex any time he wanted it, but *she* was the woman he wanted. A warm glow of purely female pride took the chill off Caitlin's heart.

They arrived beside their cars. Her little Mazda looked like a child's toy next to David's powerful Ferrari. He had made her feel like a child this morning. He probably thought she could be manipulated as easily as one, too. He was about to learn differently.

Caitlin took her car-keys out of her bag.

David produced his out of his pocket. 'I'll drive you,' he said. 'We can come back for your car later.'

'No, thank you. That would put me under an obligation to you and I don't care for that position, David.' She proceeded to unlock her door. 'You can come with me in my car, if you like. Or do as you please,' she added with studied carelessness.

He hesitated. Caitlin could feel his tension as he decided on what move to make. She was well aware of the dilemma she had pushed him into. He wanted her with him. He hated not being in control.

'Will you drive me back here after we've done what needs doing?' he asked.

His voice was smooth but Caitlin could read the calculations in his mind. If he performed well with her parents, she would be in a more mellow mood and they could use the room her father had vacated. After that, he expected her to come back to work for him and then everything would be rosy again. The pain of being a passenger in a Mazda 121 was relatively trivial. To David, the end result would be worth it.

'Yes,' she said, silently vowing she would put him through so many revolutions he wouldn't know if he was coming or going.

He rounded the bubble car and climbed into the passenger-seat with some difficulty. It was a little car. He was a big man. He settled himself without complaint, proving he was a very big man.

Caitlin smiled to herself as she set off on the road to Wyong.

Not everything his way, she thought with satisfaction.

CHAPTER SEVEN

FOR the first time, Caitlin found a problem with her darling little feminine car. She felt crowded in it with David sitting beside her. His presence was highly distracting. It generated a sense of intimacy, or memories of intimacy that she could well do without at the moment. It was paramount that she keep her head, protect her heart, and glue her eyes to the road. She was quite certain of the order of priorities, so she attempted all three at once.

'You'd better fill me in on what the situation is with your family,' David suggested reasonably. It was somewhat goading that he could *appear* to be reasonable when he obviously wasn't.

'You made an impact on my father without knowing anything,' she said drily. 'Maybe we should keep it that way.'

'I'm much better with a brief,' he argued.

'Spontaneity has a lot going for it.'

He sighed.

Caitlin considered the task ahead of her. Her mother had to be pacified. If David didn't know what was happening beyond the general scheme of things, he could hardly put a foot wrong. He would be obliged to speak in soothing generalisations.

She gave him a brief synopsis.

'This morning my father walked out on my mother. Their marriage is at crisis point. Today is their wedding anniversary. Tonight my sister and I are supposed to be giving them a party to celebrate their thirty years together.' She gave him a derisive look. 'The problem is to get them back together again. For at least one more night.'

A dark blue blaze of purpose hit her eyes and held them captive before she hastily remembered they were supposed to be riveted on the road. 'Only for tonight,' he mocked.

Caitlin wrenched her gaze away and concentrated fiercely on the road in a desperate effort to block out all the nights she'd shared with David... the passion, the pleasure, the intense possession of each other.

'It's a start,' she said tightly. 'What we really need is a solution, David.'

'Why did your father walk out?'

'You'd better ask him.'

David sighed again.

Caitlin felt compelled to give a tiny bit more explanation. 'I'm sure they love each other. It's a matter of dealing with each other's needs in a way that will keep them both satisfied,' she concluded.

'Absolutely,' David agreed. 'Satisfy each other's needs. It's the first step!' He appeared to be contented with this general proposition.

'There are a lot of needs after the first step,' Caitlin reminded him.

'I'm sure there are,' he said blithely.

'David, there is more to life than sex,' Caitlin grated.

'I wasn't talking sex. I was talking loneliness.'

'You've never been lonely in your life,' she scoffed.

'How can you be so sure?'

'I know how your mind works.'

'I doubt that you do.' His face was unusually serious.

'When was the last time you were lonely?' Caitlin asked in disbelief.

'I'm glad you asked. It's the first time in our association that you've ever asked me how I felt about anything!'

It was a valid point. She never had. Not directly. She hadn't wanted David to think she was prying. Or demanding. Or nagging in a way he would find an intolerable invasion of his privacy.

Caitlin was suddenly jolted into a reappraisal of her own attitude throughout their relationship. She had let herself be intimidated by the fact that David was so eligible, and so attractive to other women. In trying not to put a foot wrong, had she stultified a natural progression? Had she herself unwittingly drawn restrictions in being too cautious, desperately wanting to please and not to offend? She had certainly taken her cues from him. Had he also taken cues from her?

'I'm sorry,' she said, deeply disquieted by her train of thought. 'I'd like to know when you were lonely.'

'Most of my life.'

This was so unexpected, it shook Caitlin. She looked her disbelief.

'Keep your eyes on the road.'

'Sorry.'

'The office felt very empty without you, Caitlin,' he added.

And her future had looked very bleak without him. 'Why do people fall in love?' she blurted out, then wished she hadn't. It was too revealing.

'It's a force of nature. One can love. One can hate. There's not much in between. Perhaps one can learn to be indifferent.'

'That's fine,' she assented quickly. It was about the only thing they had agreed on all day.

'What position have you adopted, Caitlin?' He was nothing short of direct.

'I'm a fast learner,' she replied. She *wasn't* going to make herself vulnerable by spilling out the *truth*.

They passed Wyong High School. Schoolchildren were spilling out into the streets everywhere. Buses were collecting them as Caitlin negotiated her way through the township. It was probably a good time to arrive. If Michelle had been holding her mother's hand, she would have left to make sure her six-year-old arrived home safely from school.

Caitlin parked her car in the street outside her parents' house. 'This is it,' she said, nodding to the two-storey brick home that faced the river.

'Nice position,' David observed.

'Not for my dad,' Caitlin reminded him.

'I'm coming with you,' David declared.

Caitlin had an attack of doubt about that course of action. Her mother, in a full flight of temper, could make a fire-eating dragon look tame. David would be meeting her mother for the first time. First impressions might be unfairly off-putting.

'Maybe it's better if I go alone.'

'I promised your dad I'd be with you to the end.'

She wasn't sure he had promised any such thing at all. 'Well,' she said hesitantly, 'let me do the talking.'

'It's your mother,' he readily acceded.

'As long as that's agreed...' she dubiously surrendered.

They alighted, took the path to the front door. Caitlin rang the bell to alert her mother in case she had visitors, then used her key. Caitlin suspected that her mother wasn't receiving visitors today.

'It's Caitlin, Mum,' she called as she ushered David into the foyer.

There was a splendid arrangement of red roses on the console table. Tinsel streamers ran from the central light pendant to the walls, pinned by glittery red hearts. The party decorations hadn't come down yet, which gave Caitlin cause for hope.

She had anticipated correctly. Michelle had left. There were no visitors. Her mother was in the kitchen, chopping carrots with the deadly action of a guillotine slicing off heads. She was clearly in fine fettle. Her opening remarks set the tone of her meeting.

'Well, Caitlin, I see you've finally arrived. What took you so long to get here?'

Then she saw David.

'How could you bring a stranger into our home at a time like this?' Her voice shook with injury and outrage. 'You always did take after your father's side of the family, Caitlin. Totally insensitive!'

'I know you haven't met David, Mum...David Hartley...but you do know I've been working for him and he offered to help.'

'How can he help?' her mother snapped. 'No one can help. Your father is off hiding somewhere. I'll find him. Have no doubt about that.'

'We've been talking to Dad, Mum. Everything...'

'Where is he?'

More carrots fell to the steady tempo of the deadly weapon.

'Not far from here.'

A flurry of accelerated blows.

'So, you're not going to tell me. It's a conspiracy, is it?'

'Mum, I'm trying to sort this out. Find out what went wrong.' Caitlin closed in on her mother. 'Give me a hug.'

'Watch the knife,' David warned.

Eileen Ross threw David a glare of scornful contempt.

Caitlin managed to sidle into her mother's embrace. 'We all love you, Mum.'

A strangled cry of distress. 'Don't remind me of it, Caitlin. Your father is a rotter. That's all the thanks I get for thirty years of devoted service!'

'Dad doesn't mean it.'

'Of course he means it.'

'If you forgive him this…uh…temporary lapse, everything will be all right.'

'No, it won't,' her mother declared with determination.

'Please calm down, Mum.'

Her mother did not calm down. Caitlin did manage to persuade her into stopping the carrot-cutting and sitting down. The three of them sat around the kitchen table in a semblance of togetherness, but that was all Caitlin managed. It didn't matter what she said, or tried to say, her mother's fury with her father remained unabated. Not even for the sake of appearances would she accept her husband back for the party. He had walked out. He was in the wrong. The wound to her feelings was so great she couldn't—wouldn't— see past it.

Caitlin was getting nowhere. She looked at David for inspiration. He raised an eyebrow. She lifted both hers, and her shoulders, as well. He seemed to take it as some kind of cue.

'Caitlin, we need action,' he stated decisively.

It wasn't what she wanted to hear.

'I think we should leave,' he went on.

'You've only just got here,' Mrs Ross stated in surprise. 'Why would you want to leave?'

'Because you're wasting Caitlin's time. You're wasting my time,' he continued uncharitably. 'Most of all because you're wasting your own time, Mrs Ross,' he said more significantly, his dark blue eyes simmering with more than impatience.

David rose from the chair on the other side of the kitchen table, strode around to Caitlin, took her hands in his and drew her to him. Caitlin was so depressed and depleted of energy that she limply allowed him to press her hands against his chest.

'You've done your best, Caitlin,' he assured her with throbbing conviction. 'No one could have done more. I'm impressed.'

'What does this mean?' her mother asked suspiciously, immediately alert to the nuances.

It was David's turn to look surprised. 'Caitlin and I are lovers, Mrs Ross. Hasn't she told you yet?'

The top of Caitlin's head blew off. At least, that was how it felt. Her brain was an empty scramble of horror, a void so deep it was bottomless.

'Oh, my God!' her mother gasped, clasping her heart.

David riveted his attention on Caitlin, apparently unaware he had just exposed her to a continuing nightmare of censure from her mother for years to come. 'If your parents want to have a spat, Caitlin, that's their business. Nothing to do with us. You wanted to spend the day making love. At least we can have the night. Let's get back to Sydney.'

'Caitlin, tell me this isn't true!' her mother cried. 'It can't be true!'

'Well, no, of course it's not true,' Caitlin agreed in agitated appeasement. 'Not really.'

'I brought you up to be a good girl.'

'Oh, she is good,' David said, warming to his subject and bringing it to the boil. 'Very, very, very good. I have no complaints whatsoever. You've done a great job, Mrs Ross.'

'Caitlin!' Her mother fought for breath. 'The scandal! How could you do this to us?'

'I've put a stop to it, Mum.' It was a plea for extenuating circumstances. She snatched her hands from David's in a wild effort to establish a proper distance between them.

'Too late,' David chimed in with wicked unconcern. 'Far too late.'

Her mother rose to her feet, quite majestic in delivering her judgement. 'Caitlin, this is serious!'

'Yes, Mum,' Caitlin said weakly. The world had suddenly changed and it appeared she was to be the victim.

'Get your father home. Immediately. You are not to take no for an answer. It's his place to deal with this matter. After all, you are his daughter.'

She glared at David. 'When my husband hears about this, you'll be in deep trouble.'

'I'm sure I will be.'

'You have abused your position as my daughter's employer. You'll have a lot to answer for, young man.'

Caitlin's mind whirled again. She felt weak. Very weak.

'Don't stand there gawking, Caitlin,' her mother commanded. 'You know where your father is. Get him home straight away. I want answers.'

'Yes, Caitlin,' David blithely urged. 'You go and get your father. I'll stay and tell your mother what's really been going on. I wish to make a clean breast of it and confess everything.'

That shocked Caitlin's brain back into action. '*No, you won't.*' Inspiration struck. She snatched her car keys from the table where she'd dropped them earlier and slapped them into David's hand. 'You go and get Dad. Confess to him what you've done to me.'

'This is dangerous. Do you really want me to drive your car?'

'The car won't kill you! Dad might.'

'You'd better give me some instructions,' he advised.

'I'll certainly do that!' Caitlin said with feeling.

She followed him out, shutting the front door behind them before giving vent to pent-up passion. 'How dare you? You were the one who insisted that any intimacy we had be kept absolutely secret because of your employer/employee relationship rule. Now, here you are, telling the world!'

'Only your parents,' he corrected.

'That's worse than telling the world!'

'Your father's coming home. Your mother wants him here. You've got what you wanted.'

'And I pay for it!' she yelled at him.

'Someone has to,' he suggested mildly. 'It's a fundamental law of nature.'

'Why me?'

'Because you are sensitive and care deeply about the things you care about. Because you have a lot of love bottled up inside you trying to get out. Because you want your father and mother to be happy. Because...'

'Does it have to be this way?' Caitlin groaned.

'It is a solution, isn't it? They'll be reunited with a common purpose.' He grinned at her. 'Me!'

'Did you have to do it like that?' she wailed.

'Blood is thicker than water.' The grin grew wider. 'You asked me to be spontaneous. I was being spontaneous.'

Before Caitlin could think of a suitable reply, she was in his arms, his mouth had found hers, and the piercing ache of desire she always felt with him had descended upon her. His tongue found hers to incite and inflame and arouse. She moaned and responded, helplessly, hopelessly, cravenly wanting to blot out everything else that had happened today.

His head lifted away from hers. His fingers stroked down her hair and cheek. She could see the passion in his eyes.

'It's best when it's spontaneous.'

It left Caitlin speechless.

The big man climbed into her little bubble car. 'Don't worry about a thing, Caitlin. I'll be back.'

She watched him drive away. There was only one thing she was sure of. She hadn't got rid of David Hartley. Not from her head. Not from her heart. Not from her life.

CHAPTER EIGHT

WHERE were they?

Caitlin tried to crush the rising tide of panic that threatened to overwhelm her. Hours had passed. The first guests were due to arrive soon. David and her father should have been back long ago. Neither had arrived!

She had everything on track as far as the party was concerned. It had been action stations the moment she had come inside after seeing David off on his mission. She had rung Michelle to let her know that everything was going ahead. She had whisked her mother off to the hairdresser, insisting that she deserved to be pampered. She had made trays of *hors d'oeuvres*. Everything else for the sit-down celebratory dinner had been prepared beforehand.

Caitlin had expected her father and David to be home before her mother returned from the hairdresser. They weren't. She had bustled her mother into the bedroom to get dressed, doing her utmost to ignore a twinge of alarm. They couldn't possibly have had an accident. There had to be another explanation.

Michelle turned up with the pumpkin soup in a crock-pot, and all the ingredients for the smoked salmon and salad entrée in plastic containers. She wore a smile of supreme satisfaction that ordinarily would have made Caitlin very suspicious. In latter years, Michelle had begun to remind Caitlin of a Siamese cat. She was tall, slender, and moved with a slow, supple, feline grace. The blue eyes she had inherited from their mother and her short, sleek, ash-blonde hairstyle seemed to add to the effect.

Caitlin, however, had no time for suspicion at the present moment. The meat had to be put in the ovens, vegetables for the main course designated to various pots and pans, and plates stacked in the handiest places for serving. Above and beyond her concentration on practicalities, was a cloud of simmering apprehension.

The impulse to telephone The Last Retreat to garner what information she could was almost becoming an obsessive need. Had David arrived at the lodge? If not, what had happened to her beautiful little bubble car? She did not wish to dwell on what might have happened to David.

Yet if her mother discovered her making enquiries as to her father's whereabouts, everything could blow apart again. The newly found need for her father to deal with problems her mother couldn't deal with herself, so strongly evoked by Caitlin's fall from grace, could easily flounder.

'Where's Dad?' Michelle asked casually, apparently without a care in the world.

'Busy,' Caitlin replied abruptly, attempting to put an end to this line of questioning as quickly as possible.

'I'll bet he doesn't turn up,' Michelle said. 'He'll leave Mummy to fend for herself and be humiliated in front of everyone.'

'No, he won't,' Caitlin insisted. 'He's not like that.'

'At least Mummy had the good sense to keep control of the money.'

'She's always done that. Don't make a mountain out of a molehill, Michelle.'

Caitlin was beginning to feel more beleaguered by the minute. She wished she could use the phone. Perhaps there had been an accident on the way back from the lodge and her father was lying helpless and injured by the road. Like Dobbin this morning.

Caitlin shuddered at the thought. She had to find out what was happening.

Her mother came downstairs to supervise what was going on in the kitchen. After all, her reputation was at stake tonight and everything had to be done perfectly.

'You look lovely, Mum,' Caitlin quickly complimented her, desperate to avert a cross-examination.

Besides, her mother did look lovely. She wore a lilac silk dress, artfully draped to soften the heavier curves of her mature figure. She was still a very good-looking woman, no age pouches around her blue eyes, her skin relatively unwrinkled even on her neck. She wore several gold chains that emphasised her femininity. Her hair was dyed to a light golden blonde and fluffed around her face in a very becoming style. It took years off her actual age.

Unfortunately, Caitlin's compliment did not bring forth a smile. Her mother was clearly far too tense to smile. 'Where's your father?' she demanded to know. 'He should have been back by now.'

'He's coming,' Caitlin defended.

'He probably doesn't dare come back,' her mother said broodingly. 'Not even to deal with you, Caitlin.'

'He'll be here, Mum,' Caitlin replied with far more confidence than she felt.

'Why is Dad coming back to deal with Caitlin?' Michelle asked.

'Don't worry about it,' said Caitlin between clenched teeth. She picked up a tray. 'You could take these *hors d'oeuvres* into the lounge-room now, Mum. I must dash upstairs and change into something decent, Michelle. Won't be long.'

Caitlin bolted up the stairs and into her parents' bedroom to use the phone there. She rang The Last Retreat. The only information she could elicit was that the two men had left the lodge and the unit was vacant.

She deliberated about ringing the two local hospitals. She suppressed the impulse. If either her mother or Michelle picked up the phone downstairs while she was speaking to a hospital, pandemonium might break out.

Besides, David had said he'd be back. Caitlin clung to the fact that David was rigid about keeping to a schedule. Even when he was almost bursting with desire, as he'd been this morning, he would not let anything delay him from doing what he was set on doing. Her father would have told him what time they had to be here for the party. David would surely get them both here. It was built into his character. For the first time in her four months with him, Caitlin found comfort in David's rigid schedule-keeping.

She scooted into the bedroom set aside for her and hunted through the wardrobe for something to wear. The suitcase she had packed was still in her Mazda. At the rate time was passing, she couldn't afford to wait any longer. Apart from that, she had to make good her excuse for coming upstairs.

The wardrobe mostly contained clothes that were years old and out of fashion, but occasionally useful during weekend visits to her parents. Caitlin sighed as she thought of the smart blue cocktail dress Michelle was wearing. She pulled out a black crêpe pantsuit that would have to do and found an old pair of bronze strappy sandals that could go with it.

There was no time for proper make-up. She didn't have any anyway because of the missing suitcase. She found a tube of red lipstick in a drawer and dashed some on. It gave her a bit of colour.

She hurried back to the kitchen where she found her mother instructing Michelle that carrots could be added to the menu. There were quite enough of them. It sounded ominous.

Her mother swung around to target Caitlin. 'You were gone a long time.'

'Cramps in my stomach,' Caitlin muttered.

'Nerves,' her mother diagnosed. 'And no wonder with all the trouble you are causing, Caitlin.'

'What trouble is that?' asked Michelle.

'Don't worry about it,' Caitlin snapped. 'Where's your husband, Michelle? He's supposed to be looking after the drinks.'

'Trevor will be here as soon as he's settled the children with the babysitter. I'll say one thing for my husband against all others. He is totally dependable.'

'So is...' Caitlin bit down on her tongue. She didn't want to mention David in front of her mother.

Eileen Ross muttered dark thoughts.

Trevor came in, making the most timely entrance he had ever made! He was a local solicitor and inclined to a sense of his own importance. He took the floor immediately, demanding to be shown what he had to do to please his mother-in-law. Obviously he would not have willingly done something so menial for anyone else.

Eileen led him to the lounge-room. Caitlin grabbed the dishes of nuts and olives and followed them. It was barely twenty minutes before the party was supposed to begin. Caitlin desperately hoped David hadn't taken the concept of spontaneity too much to heart. Dependability was much more important right now.

Trevor took over the bar. He was dressed for the part in black trousers, white shirt, black bow-tie, red cummerbund. He exuded jovial confidence in carrying out his mother-in-law's instructions.

Caitlin placed the nuts and olives on top of the bar, and was glancing around to see what else needed to be done when she heard the thrum of a powerful engine coming up the driveway to the house.

'David's Ferrari!' she cried in an ecstasy of relief.

'Who's David?' Trevor asked.

'Unfortunately, you'll find out,' her mother snapped. 'Very soon.'

'He's probably pretty fast if he has a Ferrari,' Trevor remarked reasonably.

'Worse,' Eileen Ross declared with disapproving asperity. 'He's depraved.'

'Where's the Ferrari?' Michelle asked, coming in with a cheese dip and crackers.

'Dad's here!' Caitlin declared triumphantly. 'I told you he'd come. They're here now.'

An expectant silence fell in the lounge-room. Caitlin saw her mother stiffen. There was no time for a big showdown—thank heaven!—but the reception was obviously going to be frosty. For both parties. David was no more welcome than Caitlin's father. Her father had kept her mother waiting so long... Caitlin hoped they had a very good excuse for whatever had happened. She crossed her fingers.

They heard the front door open, footsteps on the slate floor of the foyer, the low murmur of voices.

'We're in the lounge-room, Dad,' Caitlin urged them on, breaking some of the nerve-tearing suspense.

Silence.

Caitlin could almost hear her father taking a deep breath. Her own heart was thumping. She expected his was, too.

More footsteps, and...the door opened.

Caitlin couldn't believe her eyes. Her father...and David...both dressed in dinner suits! Her father, who'd never worn a formal dinner suit in his life! And he looked...so distinguished and handsome...tears blurred Caitlin's eyes.

To complete the stunning contrast to his appearance this afternoon, his face was cleanly shaven, his grey hair neatly cut and groomed, his shoulders back, his carriage straight, his whole bearing and demeanour full of dignity and a readiness to meet whatever challenge he had to meet head-on.

In one hand he held a beribboned corsage of white rosebuds and baby's breath. In the other he held a white basket containing three beautifully wrapped gifts. An elaborate St Valentine's Day card was closely attached to the basket.

His first words were magnetic, focused completely on his wife. 'I love you, Eileen.'

'Henry...' Her mother's voice was almost unrecognisable, weak and wavering with a flood of feeling.

He took a tentative step forward. 'There's never been any other woman in my life except you.'

'Oh, Henry!' Her eyes shone with tears. She clasped her heart with trembling hands.

It gave Henry Ross courage. He began to walk slowly towards his wife. 'You look beautiful tonight, Eileen. I wish to always remember you like this. You're more beautiful than when we married thirty years ago.'

'I've never seen you so handsome, Henry,' her mother said, somewhat awed, certainly surprised, and almost girlishly shy.

He lifted his arms as though offering her the gifts, then stunned them all by beginning to sing in his clear tenor voice which had been unmatched in these parts for many a long year.

'Drink to me only, with thine eyes,
And I will pledge with mine...'

He moved closer, his arms enfolding his wife, drawing her to him, his eyes caressing hers as he sang on in a softer, more intimate tone.

'Or leave a kiss but in a cup
And I'll not look for wine.'

The last word lingered on a throb of deep feeling. Eileen bit her lips. Her throat moved convulsively. She had been rendered speechless, her eyes swimming with tears.

Henry took a deep breath. 'About today, Eileen,' he said pleadingly. 'I wish to explain. I had trouble with my heart after we put Dobbin down. I didn't want to alarm you...'

It instantly evoked alarm. 'Henry, you should have told me. You should have gone to the hospital immediately...'

'You know I don't like hospitals, Eileen. People die in hospitals.'

'Henry,' her voice wobbled, 'you'll be the death of me.'

'I love you, Eileen.'

'I know that, Henry.'

'After I rested for a while, I felt better. I made Caitlin promise not to tell you about my heart because I realised then you'd be angry with me for not telling you.'

David had to have coached him, Caitlin thought. Her father had been miserable, lonely and depressed. He would never have thought up such an array of excuses by himself. But there was a solid ring of truth and substance to everything he was saying. It was all deliberately slanted to smooth things over. It was working. Privately, she blessed David for producing this little miracle. It was worthy of a master magician.

'You shouldn't have hid it from me, Henry.' All the hurt wasn't gone, but it was going.

'Please forgive me, Eileen. I dressed up for you and . . .' he eased back so he could present his gifts to her '. . . I hoarded all the money you gave me to buy this for you.'

Her mother had said he'd been hoarding money. Maybe he was telling all the truth, Caitlin thought dazedly.

'I want you to wear it all so everyone will know that after thirty years, you are still the bride of my heart,' her father declared.

'Oh, Henry!' Her hands unclasped and slid up over his shoulders.

They hugged and kissed and Eileen Ross was so overcome with emotion she didn't even think of how her lipstick might get smudged.

Caitlin was deeply moved. It didn't matter that David had had a hand in orchestrating the whole scene; the timing and the clothes were perfect. Her mother was pleased, God was in his heaven, and all was right with the world. The feeling that flowed between her mother and father was genuine. Despite all their differences, they loved each other.

She glanced back at David. There was a satisfied smile on his face. He caught her glance and gave her an enquiring look, as if to ask, 'Have I done what you wanted?'

She smiled back at him.

It was a mistake.

David instantly took it as an invitation and started walking purposefully towards her. Caitlin forgave him a lot for bringing her mother and father back together again, but she was well aware that, to David, it was the means to an end that had absolutely nothing to do with her parents' happiness.

To Caitlin's mind, there was a great deal more to be sorted out with David before she could happily consent to a resumption of their relationship. In fact, she was not going to resume what they'd had before. It had to be different. Both of them had to work at making it different.

The problem was, she didn't know if what David had been doing this afternoon was for the sake of expedience—to get her back at his side—or whether he was truly prepared to reassess where they were and aim for something better. Something closer. Something far more meaningful to both of them.

Her eyes flicked back to her parents. Love that could surmount every difficulty. That was what she wanted.

'Eileen...' Her father was lifting his head from their embrace. 'I'm not going to say...'

Caitlin produced the most raucous cough her throat could manage on instant notice. It was a desperate measure to stop what was surely coming. Her father was about to destroy everything by saying he was not going to say he was sorry. The successful outcome of David's coaching had gone to his head! In the triumph of the moment, he was assuming that his wife would succumb to anything!

Caitlin knew better.

The cough succeeded in distracting her father and drawing his attention to her. Fortunately he still held her mother in his arms so Caitlin was only in her father's line of vision. She made a dramatic roll of her eyes, drew her finger across her throat in a swift slicing motion, bent her head and used a chopping action with her hand on the back of her neck. Her father got the message.

Her mother lifted her head in adoring enquiry, 'What were you not going to say, Henry?'

'I'm not going to say you're anything but wonderful, Eileen,' he said lamely, then struck on some inspiration. 'But I would like you to take off those gold chains because... well...' He drew back to offer her the basket of gifts. 'I looked it up in the library, Eileen, and for a thirtieth wedding anniversary...'

'Pearls! You bought me pearls, Henry?'

The eager delight in her mother's voice meant the critical moment of danger had been successfully bypassed. Caitlin breathed a sigh of relief.

David came up behind her. His arm slipped around her waist. 'Your father got the message,' he whispered in her ear, his breath warm and disturbingly erotic.

'Only just,' she muttered back. Her father could be the very devil, once he got a bee in his bonnet.

'You have to take the credit,' David murmured. 'Your skills at sign language are definitely improving.'

She trod on his foot to keep him silent, to stop the tantalising brush of his lips close to her ear, to let him know he couldn't take too much for granted. Not with her. Not any more.

He gave a small grunt, removed his hand from her waist.

Caitlin removed her foot from his.

'OK,' said David. 'I got that message. You don't like compliments.'

Caitlin stood there in a dilemma.

David deserved a reward for what he had accomplished. She wanted to give him a reward. The difficulty was that the reward David wanted, and the reward she was prepared to give, were not one and the same thing.

She turned to him, her eyes seeking his in a painful plea for honesty. 'I do like compliments,

David. As long as there's no payment expected for them. As long as they're truly felt. And I thank you, with all my heart, for what you've achieved for my family tonight.'

'I thought only of you, Caitlin. I did it for you,' he replied, his eyes a steady blaze that burned into her heart.

'Why?' she whispered.

'I want to keep you with me,' he answered simply.

She felt disappointed in his reply. She had wanted more from him. But perhaps it was too soon to expect more. At least they were talking to each other in a way they had never talked before. It was a start towards something better.

She looked back at her parents. Her father was fastening a string of pearls around her mother's throat. Thirty years, Caitlin thought. How long does it take? she wondered. Where would she and David be in thirty years?

How long did he want to keep her with him?

For what purpose?

CHAPTER NINE

CAITLIN could not have been more satisfied with the way the party was going.

Her mother was floating on a cloud of happiness, basking in her husband's adoration, showing off the pearls he had given her to all the guests—a lovely pearl ring and ear-studs as well as the necklace—and glowing with pleasure in the shower of congratulations and good wishes.

Her father, intoxicated by his new-found power to woo his wife, continued to woo her with a gallantry that was the envy of all her friends.

David dispensed French champagne which had suddenly and mysteriously appeared from some unknown source. The pleasure of such unexpected extravagance added bubble to the party. He had certainly thought of everything. For her, Caitlin reflected with heady pleasure. He had done it all for her.

Trevor, impressed, did his best to cultivate a friendship with the man who owned a Ferrari and obviously dabbled in French champagne. He found that being the barman might still be classified as menial work in his own classification of important jobs, but it did have its compensations.

The only person who was not happy was Michelle. 'What on earth got into Dad to act like that?' she remarked peevishly to Caitlin. 'It's not at all like him!'

'Perhaps he remembered how it once was,' Caitlin answered, her voice soft with the secret yearning to have the same feeling between her and David one day.

'He's got Mummy all moonstruck. She's behaving like a silly little girl.' This clearly did not meet with Michelle's approval.

'What's wrong with that?' Caitlin queried.

'Who's to know where it might lead?' Michelle grumbled.

Caitlin observed her sister keenly, recollecting the smug air she had thought suspicious earlier. 'Is that a problem for you, Michelle?' she asked, wondering how much her sister had contributed to the breakdown of communication between her mother and her father.

'Of course not!' Michelle snapped. 'I just think it's all very... ridiculous!' Her eyes narrowed on Caitlin. 'Are you and David Hartley at the bottom of it all?'

'I wish we were, Michelle,' Caitlin said with a warmth that showed her heartfelt approval of the romantic reconciliation.

Michelle dropped that line of conversation and they were too busy to talk much for a while. The twenty-eight guests were seated with their host and hostess at the long, beautifully decorated table that had been set up in the rumpus room. David and Trevor circled the table with bottles of wine, pouring what was requested by the guests. Caitlin and Michelle served the pumpkin soup.

Michelle opened fire again as she and Caitlin prepared the entrée. 'Who is David Hartley, anyway?'

'You know that already.'

Caitlin didn't wish to divulge the information that she had quit her position today. It was none of Michelle's business. Besides, at the rate things were happening, Caitlin couldn't discount going back to work for him. Maybe tomorrow.

'What is he?' Michelle asked tartly.

'You know the answer to that as well.'

'How much money does he have?'

'I have no idea. Why don't you ask him?'

Michelle's eyes narrowed. 'How much money does he owe on the Ferrari?'

Caitlin began to bristle. 'Five million, seven hundred and eighty-five thousand dollars and sixteen cents.'

'He might be about to go bankrupt,' Michelle said sweetly.

'I don't care.'

'People who spend their money on flashy cars and cases of French champagne often do go broke. Serves them right, too.'

Envy, Caitlin thought.

She'd never been in tune with her older sister. She suspected Michelle had married Trevor because he was a good, solid income-earner. Perhaps that was also why she stayed so close to their mother, who held the purse-strings in their family.

It was a fairly hefty purse since the sale of the farm. Caitlin didn't like this train of thought but she couldn't dismiss it.

They cleared the table of the soup-plates, started cooking the baked vegetables, then served the entrée. Her mother and father were having a wonderful time. Trevor was assiduously keeping glasses filled. Caitlin wondered if they would have to hire a fleet of taxis to take everyone home when the party was over. The atmosphere was very merry.

David had appointed himself disc-jockey and was playing guests' requests from her parents' collection of old-time songs. He didn't seem to mind, being here with her family, solving their problems, contributing to their pleasure. He grinned at Caitlin, as though he was really enjoying himself. It made her feel happy. She couldn't stop herself from smiling back at him before returning to the kitchen.

Once dinner was over, she would make the opportunity to ask David about his family. His claim that he had been lonely for most of his life seemed to indicate a long lack of close relationships. Perhaps that was the reason for his reticence on the subject, and also why he drove himself so hard to be successful at business. It filled in what he missed out on in other areas of his life.

Now that David had opened the door for her to ask him about his feelings, Caitlin decided she could satisfy herself about a lot of things that had frustrated her in the past. She could hardly put more of a step wrong than when she had walked out on him this morning. His subsequent response to that action proved she could take more steps than she had ever dreamed possible.

Her heart felt particularly light as she emptied the dishwasher of the soup-plates, ready to load in the entrée plates. She put the clean crockery away on its shelf in the walk-in pantry, collected the carving dishes for the legs of pork and lamb, and set them on the kitchen bench.

Michelle made the gravy and put it aside to be heated again later. With their schedule right up to the minute, Michelle took the opportunity to peck at Caitlin again.

'Why has Dad got to deal with you? What about?'

Caitlin gritted her teeth. She was sick of Michelle's peevish mood. If the burr under her sister's skin was frustrated curiosity, perhaps the best thing to do was give her something she could really chew on. She turned to Michelle with a careless shrug.

'Oh, Mum found out that I'm having an affair with David.'

Michelle's mouth dropped open. Her eyes whirled with the thought that Caitlin might have found herself a better deal with David Hartley than she had with Trevor. It was unacceptable.

'You're not!' she jeered in disbelief.

'I most certainly am! And what's more...' Caitlin advanced on Michelle to shove her enviable situation right down her sister's throat '...I am enjoying it to the hilt!'

It was only a little white lie, Caitlin reflected, and it couldn't possibly do any harm.

'Darling!'

The impassioned endearment that seemed to break over Caitlin's head stunned her into utter stillness. It was David's voice! He'd heard what she'd said to Michelle!

There was a crash of stacked plates being dumped on the tiled bench-top behind her. Strong hands grasped her waist and drew her against him. Warm lips descended on her bare shoulder. 'Let's make love immediately,' he intoned with heated fervour. 'I need you so badly. I've waited so long. You're so beautiful.'

'Good grief!' Michelle cried in stricken horror. She spun on her heel. 'Trevor! Trevor, come here at once! Get Dad! Get Mum! There's a mad rapist in the kitchen.'

'It worked,' David said with some elation. 'Now, quickly, Caitlin, into the pantry...'

Before Caitlin could collect her wits she was in the pantry.

'...and lock the door,' David concluded triumphantly, suiting his actions to his words.

'What do you think you're doing?'

'Keeping your parents happily united.'

'They don't need any more uniting!'

Her mouth was an open invitation which he immediately plundered. Caitlin closed her eyes. Her disgrace was complete. Michelle would see to that.

David was leaning against the door, his arms wrapped protectively around her, her body pressed to his, and he was kissing her with such devouring, heart-warming passion, any defences she might have raised disintegrated under the devastating impact of his lips, his tongue, his teeth, the sheer sensational power of his desire for her.

He not only left her breathless, he bound her to him with a sensual intensity that Caitlin didn't wish to fight. They had been lovers for months, and the addiction to his lovemaking was not crushed in a day. It was as though his body called to hers, arousing a compelling need for the togetherness it promised, a bonding that banished loneliness.

She strained closer. He moved his legs further apart to accommodate her, giving a more intimate contact, and she felt the hard burning heat of him seep through her thin clothes, appeasing the empty ache she had tried to ignore all day. Right or wrong, she revelled in his need for her, and she recklessly abandoned the constraints she had imposed on herself for the sake of her self-respect.

Her hands slid around his neck, her fingers thrusting through his hair, holding him to her, stroking him, loving him with a fierce, exultant love that returned kiss for kiss in an escalating frenzy of passion. His mouth moved from hers to graze erotically over her ear. 'Caitlin...Caitlin...' he breathed, as though repeating an ancient mantra inscribed on his soul.

She felt she was being drawn into a sweet swirl of deep inner thrall...a force of nature that would consume their separate lives and meld them into one being. The rest of the world was in darkness.

The nights with David had always compensated for the concerns of the days. Almost. She had sometimes wished the nights would never end.

She lifted her eyelashes. There was no light. There was only a darkness that pulsed with feeling. She closed her eyes, content that it should be so. Let all the lights of the world go out as long as she could be with David like this.

The sound of voices approaching broke into their absorption with each other. Unwelcome. Inescapable. Causing David to lift his head and listen.

'It's not the fuses,' said one.

'Well, something caused the lights to go out,' said another.

'That was you, David,' she whispered.

'Power's gone, as well,' someone else said.

'No, Caitlin. It was you,' David murmured.

'Better ring up the electricity commission. Get someone out here as quickly as possible.'

Caitlin looked at David although she didn't see him in the pitch blackness. 'How did you do it?' she whispered again.

'I?' His voice was thick with emotion, but sounded innocent.

Above the sounds of confusion and crisis arising from the other side of the pantry door, there was one voice that carried with the clarity of a ringing bell.

'How will I ever live this down? The meal is ruined!'

It was her mother's voice.

She heard David sigh.

CHAPTER TEN

THE meal was not ruined.

David took charge.

He elicited the information that this was the only house in the street without lights. He despatched Caitlin, Michelle and Trevor to the neighbours' homes with the pots and pans of vegetables. The heat in the ovens would finish cooking the meats. He persuaded her parents and their guests to resume their places at the candlelit table, poured champagne for them all, proposed a toast to the happy couple celebrating their thirtieth wedding anniversary, and instigated the speech-making that would normally have taken place after the meal.

In the meantime, the County Council arrived, diagnosed a power overload due to the number of electrical appliances being used, sent an electrician up a pole to change a transformer, and in half an hour had fixed the problem.

Henry Ross took the opportunity to sing, '*When the lights come on again...*' and the guests to join in, '*...all over the world...*' to much laughter and merriment.

Trevor was able to start the carving; the neighbours carried in the cooked vegetables and joined the party. Caitlin and Michelle served the dinners, and, since everyone's appetite was sharpened by the unscheduled delay, the meal was enjoyed all the more.

Despite the undoubted success of the rescue operation, or perhaps because of it, Michelle made it her business to tell Mummy that Caitlin and David were doing things in the pantry when the lights went out. She sweetly informed Caitlin that this was for her own good.

Trevor thought so, too. The family should not be subjected to such scandalous behaviour and it was perfectly clear that David Hartley was the kind of man who rode roughshod over everyone and anyone.

Trevor was undoubtedly piqued that he had been appointed a labourer during the crisis while David shone as a team leader.

After the sweets course and before coffee was served, her father slipped away from the dinner table and took Caitlin aside. 'Caitlin, I'd like to speak to you if I may,' he said in his mild and gentle manner.

'Sure, Dad. What about?'

'David Hartley.'

Caitlin's heart sank. 'Do you have to?'

'Your mother said I had to deal with you.'

'Well, in that case ... I suppose we'd better get it over and done with.'

'Trevor said I had to be stern with you.'

'Trevor would,' Caitlin muttered.

'And Michelle said I was to be severe. Indeed, I think the word "harshly" came into the conversation. Harshly severe.'

'Oh, dear,' Caitlin said with resignation.

'I don't see that I have any option, Caitlin. None that's viable.'

'No,' Caitlin agreed. 'You'll have to do it.'

'Perhaps it would be best if we did this privately. Could I ask you to step into the study please, Caitlin?'

'Sure, Dad.'

The study was more a room of memorabilia, her father's escape to the past. Photographs of his best horses covered the walls, along with the ribbons they had won at shows. The purple rosette for 'Supreme Champion' in the Galloway Class took pride of place. Caitlin walked over and touched it.

'I do understand how much you must miss this, Dad,' she said in soft sympathy.

'It's a loss, but your mother was right to sell up, Caitlin. The doctors said I wouldn't last if I kept up the work. When I had that queer turn this morning...'

Caitlin turned in quick concern. 'You did? You should have told me, Dad.'

'I got over it. Made me face up to a lot of things today.'

Caitlin reflected that it had been that kind of day for her, too... facing up to what she wanted and where she was going with David.

'Your mother's been trying to interest me in other things for my own good,' her father went on. 'I was being a stubborn old fool... not co-operating. Didn't want to let go. Your mother's a wonderful woman, Caitlin. Always knows best.'

'Yes, Dad,' she agreed, not wanting to throw even the tiniest spanner into the harmony that had been established between her parents. Privately, she reserved the opinion that no one had the right to decide for anyone else what was 'for their own good'.

Her father coughed. 'Well, almost always.' He gave her an intent look. 'Do you love David, Caitlin?' he asked quietly.

'Bits and pieces,' she answered with a rueful smile.

He nodded his head sagely. 'I understand.' He pulled himself erect and walked towards his daughter, put his hand gently on her shoulder. 'Don't take any notice of what anyone else says, Caitlin. Do what your heart tells you is right.'

'I try to, Dad.'

'I want you to be happy.'

'I know that.'

'There's only one thing to remember, Caitlin. "To thine own self be true".'

She put her arms around his shoulders and hugged him.

He grumped into his throat. 'That's about as severe as I can get, Caitlin.'

'You're the most wonderful dad in the whole world.'

'I have my failings.'

'We all do.'

'I've tried hard.'

Tears were shimmering in Caitlin's eyes. 'You don't have any failings for me, Dad,' she looked up at him. 'Why are people the way they are?'

'I don't know, Caitlin.'

'There's nothing I can do...'

'Yes, there is.'

'What is it, Dad?'

'Forgive them, Caitlin. All of them. They know not what they do.'

'Thanks for being so stern with me, Dad.' She kissed his cheek.

He smiled, loving her as he always had. 'God bless, Caitlin, and good luck with your David.'

He left to return to her mother. Caitlin followed him out of the study, biting her lip to hold back the floodgates of affection that were welling in her eyes for her father. He was a wonderful man.

She ran straight into David as she was crossing the foyer to the lounge-room.

'What's wrong with you?' he asked.

'Nothing!'

Caitlin quickly blinked back her tears. David looked stern, angry and deadly serious. Something had upset him. Had Michelle been stirring up trouble behind Caitlin's back? After everything David had done for the family today, it would be so dreadfully unfair if she had.

'There's one question you need to answer, Caitlin,' he clipped out, his eyes as hard as slate.

Her heart fluttered in alarm. Her nerve-endings picked up the different nuances in the tension flowing from him. This was not David, the lover.

This was David, the fighter. Something very important was on the line for him.

'What is it, David?'

Whatever was wrong, she wanted to put it right for him, just as he had put so much right for her. For better or for worse, she loved David Hartley. There were still difficulties to overcome or to negotiate around before she could feel completely satisfied with their relationship, but she had no doubt left in her mind that he was the man she wanted in her life.

The cold light of battle in his eyes suddenly flared into a blazing furnace of fury. 'I am well aware that I'm an uninvited guest at this feast, Caitlin. A gatecrasher who turned out to be useful. Too useful to spurn.'

Caitlin's heart contracted. Had her mother attacked him? 'David, *I'm* not spurning you,' she cried. Surely their kiss in the pantry was evidence enough of that.

'You did this morning, Caitlin. And who do you suppose has just walked in to join the party?'

'I don't know.'

'He came here, Caitlin. He came to your parents' home. Expecting you to be here. As you are.'

'I don't know what you're talking about, David?'

'Then let me refresh your memory. The man who stole my patents. The man who cheated his way into becoming my biggest competitor. The man who got to the German delegation before they came to me...'

He punched the words at her in seething accusation. She stared back at him in pained bewilderment, her brains scrambled with the implications of what he was saying.

'So tell me, Caitlin . . . what the hell is Michael Crawley doing at your parents' thirtieth wedding anniversary party?'

She had no idea. None at all. As far as she knew, Michael Crawley had no connection whatsoever with her family. She herself had never spoken a word to the man. She had only seen him once when she had accompanied David to a preliminary court hearing on the litigation between the two parties.

Like David, he was in his early thirties. He had left Caitlin with the impression of a very slick operator, with the morals of an alley cat. He was quite a handsome man and well aware of it. Caitlin hadn't liked his eyes. They seemed to be constantly calculating his effect on others.

'Well?' David prompted tersely.

How could she explain the inexplicable? Before she could think of a word to say, another voice intervened.

'Ah, there you are, Caitlin! My Valentine!'

Caitlin goggled at Michael Crawley. He stepped out of the lounge-room, into the foyer where she and David were standing, and didn't so much as hesitate in coming straight to her side, smiling at her as though they shared some special, private secret.

'Everything turned out wonderfully well, Caitlin,' he said in a tone of warm intimacy. 'I've been with the Germans all afternoon, thanks to you, my sweet.'

'You piece of slime!' David sliced at him.

Crawley laughed. 'You've never been a good loser, have you, Hartley?' He leaned closer to Caitlin and sniffed. 'Not wearing my perfume. I thought Beautiful was perfect for you.'

Caitlin was completely dumbstruck. She couldn't believe what was happening.

'I'll buy you some more tomorrow. Anything you like,' Crawley went on good-humouredly. 'More roses, as well. Jenny said you didn't take them with you.'

Jenny? Jenny Ashton? Was she in on this...this...? Caitlin couldn't find a word for it.

'Caitlin?' David bit out.

She looked at him in helpless appeal, appalled by the credibility Crawley was evoking with facts she couldn't dispute. The Germans, the perfume, the roses...it added up to a damning indictment of duplicity on her part.

David's eyes seared hers with burning questions. Caitlin didn't know how to begin to answer them. All she could think of was she was innocent.

'Let me give you a tip, old boy,' Crawley drawled condescendingly. 'If you want to keep a woman, don't take her for granted. And if you've been running after Caitlin today, you've left your run too late. Why don't you trot on home now? You are...shall we say...yesterday's man?'

'Is this true, Caitlin?' David grated.

'No!' she cried, finally finding voice. 'David, I swear it isn't!'

Crawley turned to her in exasperation. 'Don't tell me you've changed your mind again. What's he been promising you? More money?' His voice hardened. 'You can't play both ends against the middle, Caitlin. Besides...' his eyes glittered mockingly at David '...I doubt Hartley will forgive your disloyalty to him.'

'David, don't listen to him,' Caitlin begged.

But he had been listening. She could see him weighing what Crawley had said against all that had happened today, and the balance against her was growing in his mind.

'He's deliberately making trouble between us. Can't you see that?' she appealed.

'You didn't want me to meet with the German delegation,' David said flatly. 'You tried to stop me.'

'I wasn't thinking of them. I was thinking of us.'

'You were thinking of yourself, Caitlin. Was the decision made when I walked out on you?'

A chill ran down her spine. She was losing him. She tried desperately to reach across the gap that was yawning between them. 'David, don't do this. Don't let him poison what we have together. What we share...'

It was a mistake.

A cold mask of pride fell over his face.

'We share nothing.' He raked a scathing look over her body, then met her eyes with blazing contempt. 'I won't be tempted again.' He took her car keys out of his trouser pocket and tossed them to her.

'Get Crawley to drive you out to your car. Goodbye, Caitlin.'

It was only a couple of steps to the front door. David was there and gone before Caitlin could utter another word. The urge to run after him impelled her feet forward. She reached the door, grasped the handle, then realised any further plea was futile.

David had closed his ears to her, closed his heart to her. She had nothing new to say, nothing that might open his mind. If she threw herself upon him physically, he would cast her off. The desire she had so deliberately aroused this morning now damned her.

She heard the Ferrari growl, then roar into motion.

She leaned her head against the closed door and fought the wave of weakness that hollowed out her stomach and turned her knees to water. Crawley was behind her, watching her... Crawley, who had manipulated a scenario that smacked of conspiracy and betrayal... Crawley, who was undoubtedly gloating over the success of his machinations.

Caitlin stiffened her spine. She would not crumple into a heap of distress and despair. Not in front of Crawley. He had to be the lowest, meanest and vilest person in the human race. He also had to be faced. She had to challenge his lies. If she could draw something tangible from him, something she could take to David to prove her innocence, there was a chance that David might listen. Whatever happened, she would not crack.

She turned, standing right in front of the door to block Crawley's ready exit. He was watching her, a self-satisfied smirk on his face. Caitlin abhorred physical violence, but she felt such a surge of hatred for Crawley that she barely quelled the impulse to step forward and slap the evil smugness from his face.

Almost instantly she realised he would like that. His dark, greedy eyes were feasting on the effect he was having on her, enjoying his power to stir responses that weakened his opponent while he remained in control. Caitlin fiercely determined he would get no more sadistic satisfaction from her.

'Why?' she asked. 'What gain is there in this for you?'

He laughed. 'Anything that hurts Hartley is a gain for me. The more I mess up his mind, the better. Tonight I hit a bonanza. I got the jackpot.'

The relish in his voice was sickening. Caitlin eyed him with contempt. 'You have a strange idea of a bonanza.'

'Not at all. I knew Hartley was laying you. I wish him joy in living off the memory.' His eyes flicked lecherously over her curves. 'But for Hartley to actually be emotionally involved ... that I didn't expect. Nice, gut-gnawing stuff.'

David was right. Crawley was a piece of slime.

He laughed again. 'My Valentine's Day investment really paid off. Hartley must have burned at the thought of you having another lover. Wish I could have been a fly on the wall when he blew up about it.'

'He didn't blow up.'

He wagged a finger at her. 'Don't try to deceive me, Caitlin. You didn't resign for nothing. I know more about you than you know yourself.'

'How do you know I resigned?' she asked sharply.

'I know everything.'

'How did you get here?'

'I just walked in. I met an eminently bedworthy blonde who asked me to stay when I told her that I'd come about David Hartley.'

Michelle! She'd probably been hovering in the foyer to see what resulted from Daddy's talk! Another violent urge hit Caitlin. The thought of wringing her sister's neck hovered in her mind. No doubt Michelle had self-righteously decided that Caitlin should get her come-uppance for playing fast and loose with two men.

'Well, now you've had your fun, let me show you out, Mr Crawley,' Caitlin said tightly, opening the door and stepping aside to let him make his exit. 'You're not welcome here.'

'Why don't you come and work for me now you're out of a job? We could make music together.'

'Get knotted,' she said as curtly as she could.

He laughed patronisingly.

The urge to lose her temper was well nigh irresistible. The urge to assault him physically was well nigh irresistible. Caitlin fought the urges down. Both would be mistakes. Her attempts to hurt him would simply amplify his pleasure.

Where was Michael Crawley vulnerable? The answer came to her immediately. His overwhelming ego.

'You've been very clever, Mr Crawley.'

'Indeed, I have.' He was supremely confident. 'A good hand played with masterful strokes.'

Caitlin felt the bile in her stomach churning.

'Tell me how you found out about David and me, when no one else knew?'

'I think not.'

'Impress me, Mr Crawley. Or was it just a fluke?' That stung his pride. 'Of course not.'

'How, then?'

'I've had you both under surveillance.'

So simple, so obvious, once one thought of it.

'I don't believe you.' She was grasping at straws. He smirked. 'Please yourself.'

'If you had us under surveillance, you would know David's habits.'

The smirk widened. 'Oh, I do.'

'What time did he leave my apartment?'

'Six forty-five. Every time he laid you.'

The thought that Crawley knew every time they had loved each other—it was so sick—Caitlin gagged. She quickly forced out some words to cover her reaction. 'And what did David do with his schedule after that?' Caitlin didn't know herself, and it didn't matter.

Michael Crawley began to laugh, a raucous belly-filled laugh of absolute delight. 'He went to have breakfast with his mother.' The merriment shook his frame until tears of glee rolled down his eyes.

He managed to contain himself. 'You see, Caitlin, it's that piece of knowledge I'll use to destroy David Hartley psychologically. Isn't that funny? Aren't you amused? Are you impressed?'

Caitlin was going to be sick. She needed more words. Fast. 'You're a sadist, Mr Crawley.'

'Indeed I am, Caitlin.'

She swallowed hard and gestured to the open doorway. 'Goodbye, Mr Crawley.'

He strolled to the door and paused, his eyes glittering exultantly into hers. 'Think about it, Caitlin. Hartley didn't trust you. Give me a call if you want a job. I'll pay you more than he did. And revenge is sweet.'

'Yes,' she forced out. 'Yes, it is.' Somehow, some way, she would bring Michael Crawley down for what he'd done tonight.

'I'm glad we understand each other. Goodnight, Caitlin.'

He didn't wait for a reply.

She stepped out into the fresh air after him, watched him depart, then vomited over the balcony on to the garden below. She cleaned her mouth with water from the garden tap and braced herself to go back inside. It wasn't easy. She felt very shaky.

She closed the front door behind her and leaned back against it, shuddering. Michael Crawley was a venomous snake. She desperately needed an antidote for his poison. But what? The worst of it was he had spoken the truth. David's trust in her had been destroyed.

Her gaze wandered aimlessly around and struck the decorative red hearts pinned to the walls to hold the streamers. Tears welled up in her eyes. Some Valentine's Day this had been! Michael Crawley was as deadly as Al Capone. He might as well have machine-gunned her heart. She felt as though she was bleeding to death.

Then the strains of the music being played in the lounge-room impinged on her consciousness. The tune was hauntingly familiar, drawing her into listening for the words. One phrase was all she needed to hear. Recognition hit her like another wound to her heart—the theme song from the movie, *Ghost*— 'Unchained Melody'.

It was so beautiful, expressing such a deep, yearning love . . . a love that could no longer be fulfilled in this life, yet a love that would go on burning forever. Was she doomed to be cut off from David before they had ever fully expressed what they meant to each other, wrenched apart by the evil of another man?

Her father's voice joined that of the singer, drawing Caitlin to the doorway. Through a haze of tears, she saw her parents dancing together, gazing into each other's eyes as though there was no one else in the world. Her mother started singing, too.

As Caitlin watched her parents slowly circling the floor, so touchingly in tune with each other after all these years, she vowed she would win back David's trust. And his love. It was not impossible and she wouldn't let it be.

She needed him.
She wanted him.
She would have him.
He, too, had been lonely most of his life.

CHAPTER ELEVEN

CAITLIN arrived at the office at eight o'clock. The cleaning staff was packing up, ready to leave. She presented Michael Crawley's roses to one of the women, the basket of gifts to another. She borrowed a can of air-freshener to get rid of the scent of roses. As far as was possible she eliminated the loathsome reminders of that poisonous man.

She found her letter of resignation still on her desk. She left it there. She found a message on the fax machine that probably spelt death to her hopes, but there was nothing she could do about it. She left it there. She went to the ladies' room. Her need to go was working overtime this morning. Her mother was right about nerves. Caitlin had never felt so nervous in her life.

She checked her appearance again, fretting over her choice of clothes. Maybe she should have worn the green dress David liked. But he might remember he had complimented her on it and think she was trying to be seductive. She had selected the red suit because it was a bold colour and she needed to be bold this morning. Unfortunately it had the effect of showing up the pallor of her face, the obvious sign of strain and fatigue.

It had been a long night. She had covered David's departure by simply saying he had to return to

Sydney. She had let Michelle and Trevor and her mother interpret that any way they liked. When the party had ended, she had driven two of the guests home to Yarramalong, and they were so appreciative of the favour that they didn't mind her driving their car on to The Last Retreat and leaving it there so she could pick up her bubble car.

On the drive back to Sydney she hadn't felt constrained to keep up a happy façade, but there had been no relief for her churning mind. She'd had only minimal patches of sleep in the few hours left before she had to rise for an early start to work. She wondered if David had fared any better. Did he have any doubts about his decision to leave her with Michael Crawley?

She puzzled over what Crawley had said about David's mother as she returned to her office. How could he use the fact that David breakfasted with his mother every morning to his advantage? It made no sense to her. Some derogatory comment about David's being a Mummy's boy was surely all he could get out of it. That wouldn't wash far. David was clearly not the kind of wimp the term suggested.

Yet why was David so assiduous in keeping to that schedule? Did his mother have some kind of hold on him? How did such constant contact with his mother tie in with the loneliness he had supposedly known? Why hadn't he ever taken Caitlin home with him?

So many questions that needed answering.

It was eight twenty-two when she re-entered the office. David would arrive at eight-thirty. He was a man of rigid routine. His first action would be to check if any transmissions had come through on the fax machine overnight. Which meant her office was the first stop.

Caitlin watched the minutes crawl by. She couldn't make up her mind how best to face David. Should she be sitting at her desk, or standing? Would it look presumptuous if she sat as though prepared to start a day's work? At least that would put the desk between her and David. Coward, she berated herself. He wouldn't throw her out bodily. Or would he?

Eight-thirty.

She stood behind her desk, beside her chair. To her left was her computer and printer. Behind her was the fax machine. To her right were the filing cabinets. Beyond the filing cabinets and in front of her was the door.

It started to open.

Caitlin gripped the backrest of her chair, fingers digging into the fabric. She could feel the throb of her pulse in her temples. Her heart was pumping in overdrive. Her stomach was in spasmodic revolt.

David did not stride in with his usual electric vitality. The door stood open for several moments, as though he was reluctant to enter, perhaps recoiling from any reminder of his intimate relationship with a woman who had supposedly betrayed his confidence. Then he stepped inside, grim-faced, resolute, but there was a haggard look about his eyes that spoke of lack of sleep, lack of any interest in the day ahead of him.

He stopped dead when he saw her. His body tensed. His face sharpened. His eyes blazed with anger. 'What are you doing here?' he snapped.

'I've never accepted injustice easily,' Caitlin stated, her voice trembling even though she had rehearsed the words a hundred times.

His mouth compressed. His eyes were those of a judge who had already passed sentence on a proven traitor, hard, contemptuous of any protest. He stared at her with an intensity designed to reduce her to a quivering wreck.

It had the opposite effect. A surge of adrenalin poured strength into her limbs. Her mind focused very clearly on her purpose. She stared back in unwavering challenge, armoured with her innocence.

'May I remind you . . . you resigned yesterday?' he said with deadly intent.

'Yes, and I gave you formal notification of it in a letter. You left the letter on my desk . . .' she pointed to it '. . . for anyone to walk in and see.'

She took a deep breath and plunged on. '*I* didn't tell Michael Crawley I'd resigned. *You* didn't tell Michael Crawley I'd resigned. Yet he knew, David. His act last night was based on the fact that I'd resigned.'

'Act?' he savagely mocked.

Her chin lifted. 'I don't intend to be the scapegoat for someone on your staff, who also happens to be in Michael Crawley's pocket.'

'Why should I believe it's anyone else but you, Caitlin?'

'Because I'm here, David. Fighting on your side. And if you throw me out, Crawley will have won what he wanted to win when he sent the roses and other gifts to stir trouble between us and distract concentration from the meeting with the Germans.' She paused, then added, 'I did my best to get that business deal back for you, David. You know I did.'

He weighed her argument and found it wanting. 'No one on the staff knew we were lovers, Caitlin. Your suggestion of a mole feeding Crawley information doesn't quite cover that,' he said cynically.

'It doesn't have to. Crawley has had you under surveillance. He boasted of it after you left last night. He knows what nights you spent at my apartment and precisely what time you left in the morning.'

'Why should I think that information didn't come from you?' he demanded tersely.

'You've never told me what you did after you left me in the morning, David,' she shot at him, determined to hold his attention.

'I went home, of course,' he snapped.

'You breakfast with your mother. Every morning. Without fail. And Crawley intends to use your mother against you. I was a bonus weapon to needle you. Your mother is his big gun.'

He froze. Total immobility. It was as though she had turned him to stone with her last words. His eyes went completely blank, their focus turned inward to something so critical or momentous that it obliterated all consciousness of anything else.

Caitlin's nerve-endings jangled with tension. What could produce such a reaction in him? What was the mystery about his mother? What power over him did it give Michael Crawley?

She saw David's hands clench. She sensed the fierce aggression surging through him. Then very slowly they unclenched. Control re-established. His eyes refocused on her, burning with the need to know.

'How does Crawley intend to use my mother?' His voice was flat, unemotional.

'I don't know, David,' Caitlin answered quietly. 'He laughed about it. He said he intended to break you psychologically and your mother was the key. He was gloating. It made me sick. The man is a sadist, David. He enjoys hurting others.'

He winced and looked away, but not before Caitlin saw the sickness he felt. He shook his head as though he couldn't believe, didn't want to believe what she had told him. Yet when he faced her again there was pained acceptance in his eyes.

'Thank you for sticking by me, Caitlin.' His voice was low and strained. 'God knows I've given you no reason to.'

'You helped me yesterday.'

And I love you.

Maybe the silent message showed in her eyes. He looked discomforted. Yesterday he had wanted to keep her with him, but he hadn't trusted her when put to the test. It put him in the wrong. Badly in the wrong.

'Did everything finish up right last night?' he asked.

'Very much so.' A smile fleetingly touched her lips at the memory of her mother and father dancing and singing together. 'You did a great job.'

David's mouth curled in self-mockery. 'You could say Crawley taught me a lesson.' His eyes wandered over her, not with desire, more as though he was seeing her anew. When he lifted his gaze to hers, his expression reflected some inner torment. 'I should have given you the roses.'

She looked down at the desk, disquieted by his torment. 'I guess it wasn't that kind of relationship,' she said dully, her eyes fastening on the letter of resignation.

Maybe it would never be... for him. He had kept her at a distance all along. She knew so little about him. She hadn't even known about his mother. 'You don't have to feel guilty about it, David,' she blurted out defensively. 'You didn't force me into anything I didn't want, and it's not your fault that I wanted more than you did.'

'I wasn't aware,' he said quietly. 'I'm sorry that you felt ... so ... unappreciated.'

Unloved.

Her heart clenched. Was she aiming for the impossible? She couldn't bear to look at him, to see the answer in his eyes. She stared at her signature on the letter of resignation. 'Perhaps it's best that I leave now,' she said, giving him the opportunity to state his feelings, wanting him to be honest, yet dreading it.

Silence.

Caitlin felt the whole weight of her future pressing down on her. She fiercely willed David to meet her halfway on the path towards the closeness she desperately wanted with him.

'I realise...that after last night...' he began with obvious difficulty.

Caitlin held her breath. Her mind screamed at him...*don't let me go*!

'If you can find it in your heart to give me...us...another chance, Caitlin...I want you to stay on with me,' he said, each word measured as though chosen with great care.

Caitlin's mind dizzied with relief. She breathed again. She lived again. It took her several moments to regain enough composure to lift her head and look David straight in the eye. 'I need your trust, David.'

'You have it. It will never falter again, Caitlin. That I promise you,' he answered gravely.

She wanted to ask about his mother, but was wary of pressing too far, too soon. There had to be some highly sensitive issue involved for David to have reacted in the way he had to the idea of Crawley's exploiting it. Leave well enough alone for now, she decided. She had achieved her first aim. There could be no love without trust.

'Thank you,' she said, wishing he would close the distance between them, haul her into his arms, and kiss her with all the pent-up need she felt. He looked as if he was tempted, very tempted. But they were in the office. That had always imposed restraints.

Break them! The rebellious thought burned through her mind. Then she remembered the miserable failure of her attempt to break David's schedule yesterday morning, and how it had eaten away his trust last night. An agreement was an agreement. Although she was not going to agree to it any more. If David wanted to resume a love-affair with her, the terms had to change. Love shouldn't have to remain bottled up and hidden half the time.

She forced her mind to push that issue into abeyance and concentrate on business. 'A fax came in from the German delegation. You'd better read it,' she said crisply, then turned to tear the sheet of paper out of the machine.

It would certainly test David's trust, she thought ruefully. Herr Schmidt had confirmed that he and his associates had spent yesterday afternoon talking to Michael Crawley. He didn't precisely say that any deal with the Hartley company was dead, but it was plain he expected David to woo him back to the conference table if there was to be any further talking.

She heard David coming towards her and took a few deep calming breaths before turning to hand him the page of potential dynamite. She didn't realise how close he was to her until she swung around and bumped into him. His hands surrounded her waist. To steady her? Or... ? She glanced up sharply, unaware of the flash of intense vulnerability in her eyes.

'Caitlin...' It was a raw groan. He lifted a hand to her cheek, touching it as though driven by the need to feel her skin, her flesh, her warmth. The tortured questions in his eyes were suddenly consumed by a flare of desire. His fingers raked through her hair. He scooped her body against his. Before Caitlin could catch her breath his mouth was on hers, hungry, urgent, seeking possession with a passion that would not be denied.

It was a fierce and total abandonment of his *office rules*. Caitlin did not know what had triggered it. She didn't care. It swept away all the fears and nerve-tearing tension that had made hell of the hours of loneliness. It was release, reassurance, reaffirmation of what they felt with each other, and so intense were the feelings aroused that they left little room for thought of where this might lead.

An insistent little voice in the back of her mind started beating a drum of warning. She was giving in again, demonstrating to David that she was his to take whenever he felt like it. Was she going to let him have his way with her? Suit his convenience? Wasn't this putting her back to where she was before she had walked out yesterday?

She wrenched her mouth from his, ashamed of her feverish response to his kisses. 'No,' she gasped, shaking her head out of his grasp in protest.

Her eyes flew up to his in harried confusion. He wanted her. He wanted her so much that he didn't care what any staff member who happened upon them might think. But she cared. She didn't want to be thought of as David Hartley's 'affair on the side'. It cheapened what she felt.

'David, I'm here as your assistant. Nothing else,' she declared, her green eyes fiercely challenging the power of his attraction and his expectation that she was always going to succumb to it.

'Sorry, I forgot,' he said apologetically. 'Please remind me if it happens again.' He was as unrepentant as it was possible to be.

Caitlin had the impression from the manner in which his eyes were shining at her that she might have to remind him on a regular and frequent basis.

He was still *pressing* her body to his. There was satisfaction reflected in his eyes. Caitlin rebelled against it, pushing herself out of his embrace. Only then did she see the forgotten, half-crumpled fax in her hand.

'Look at this!' she cried, shaking it at him. 'It's not good news, David.' She knew from previous incidents how he would react when he saw it. She would be forgotten.

He took the sheet and scanned the print with about as much interest as he would give to junk mail. 'Caitlin, tell them to deal with Crawley if they wish, but we're not interested in dealing with anyone who deals with Crawley.' He tossed the page into the disposal bin.

'But you...I thought...' She bit her lips. It was his decision and it was not her place to question it, yet it was such a turnaround of attitude from him.

He turned to her, his eyes ablaze with some newly born conviction. 'Crawley hurt you. He intends to hurt me. He intends to hurt...' He grimaced. 'No business is worth the cost of hurting people I care about.'

Caitlin's heart skipped a little.

'Now that's settled, Caitlin, I'm going to talk to my mother and prepare her for what's coming. I'm going home.'

Her pleasure in what had seemed real caring for her was somewhat punctured. David had claims placed on him by his mother that took priority over her. In the circumstances she shouldn't mind. But she did. After what had happened between them Caitlin needed a lot of reassurance.

'Wouldn't it be faster to ring her?' she asked.

He looked pained. 'This isn't something I wish to talk about over the phone.'

She reined in her need to know, hoping he would trust her enough to confide everything to her very soon. 'I'll take care of whatever needs taking care of,' she assured him.

His eyes softened, caressing her with a warmth that he had never shown before. 'Your father thinks the world of you. And I think your father is a fairly astute man.'

A sweet wave of heat flooded through her body. It was such a nice thing to tell her! She wasn't used to David being *nice* to her. Riveting, magnetic, dynamic, passionate... a force of nature that she had found it impossible to resist... but *nice* was definitely something new... and very heart-warming.

She mused over what this difference meant as she watched him stride to the door, his vitality restored. He paused when he reached it, as though struck by some afterthought. He looked back. She hadn't moved. The sense of the world having tilted slightly in her favour was heady stuff.

David's cobalt-blue eyes flashed with purpose. 'What kind of horse do you want, Caitlin?'

The question startled her. 'I haven't thought about it.'

'Think about it,' he commanded. 'I'll be back.' He used his fingertips to blow her a kiss.

After he had left her, Caitlin did give it thought. It conjured up a lot of ideas, a lot of feelings, a lot of dreams about the future. She made one very firm resolution. If David Hartley thought she could be bought—body, mind and soul—with a horse, he could think again. She would accept the horse. No hesitation about that. But what happened afterwards depended upon a lot of other things.

His good behaviour was one thing.

Being introduced to his mother was another!

CHAPTER TWELVE

CAITLIN spent some time composing a reply to the fax from the German delegation. She couched it in terms that left the door open for them to come back to a negotiating position with Hartley's, but stated quite clearly that if they wished to deal with Crawley, the responsibility for the consequences was theirs alone.

Caitlin felt satisfied with that. She hoped the word, 'consequences', would give pause for thought. She didn't see why Crawley should be handed the business on a platter, not after the heartache he had given both her and David yesterday. The man was a monster, without conscience or heart. She hated the thought of him winning anything.

She transmitted the reply and was in the process of filing it when a thought occurred to her. She rang Jenny at reception.

'Hi! It's Caitlin.'

'Oh, Caitlin!' Jenny sounded surprised. 'I didn't see you come in this morning,' she quickly added. 'What can I do for you?'

Caitlin's heart sank. She didn't want Jenny to be Crawley's informer. Although he had dropped Jenny's name last night, Caitlin had thought that could have been quite deliberate. It would amuse

136

Crawley to get someone who was innocent into trouble. Perhaps Jenny's excuse for being surprised was genuine. Caitlin hoped so.

'Tell me, Jenny, who came into my office yesterday after I left here?' she asked.

'Mr Hartley,' she answered promptly.

'How do you know?'

'He used your extension to dial out.'

'Who else?'

'Herr Schmidt.'

'How do you know?'

'He wanted me to get some information on entertainment. What was on at the Opera House. Things like that. He used your extension to talk to me.'

'Who else, Jenny?'

'No one.'

Caitlin paused to consider.

'Jenny, if you can't think of anyone else who might have come into my office, I think you had better come up and see me.'

A long pause.

'There was one other person,' Jenny confessed. She sounded scared.

'Who, Jenny?' Caitlin pressed.

'Me. I wanted to see the roses again,' she gushed, anxious to excuse herself. 'I saw them delivered in the morning before you arrived. They were so lovely, much nicer than the ones my boyfriend gave me. I was just a teeny bit envious. I'm sorry, Caitlin. I swear I didn't do anything. I didn't touch a thing.'

She didn't have to, Caitlin reflected. All she had to do was read her letter of resignation.

'Oh, Jenny...'

'I swear I didn't do anything wrong, Caitlin. I swear it.'

'No one else came into my office?'

'I'm certain of it. Paul Jordan came back a little before closing time. He chatted to me about his day for a few minutes, how he hoped to close a really big deal, then went home. The other salesmen filtered through. The factory manager came in, but no one else, literally no one went upstairs.'

'Thank you, Jenny.'

'Is everything OK?'

Caitlin hesitated, wishing she could let Jenny off the hook. Perhaps it was no more than an indiscretion. But such indiscretions had to be stopped. 'I'm afraid it isn't, Jenny,' Caitlin said sadly, and hung up.

The mail arrived. She dealt with it as far as she could and made preparatory notes for David's attention. Business calls came in. She took messages and made appointments.

Caitlin was so busy that she did not notice time passing. Jenny's involvement with the flow of information concerning David Hartley's business activities to Michael Crawley kept surfacing in her mind. Caitlin's own involvement with David Hartley, and what the future held, was never far from her consciousness.

When David returned to the office, his face was set in stern, unyielding lines. Implacable. Resolute.

Caitlin knew the look. Whatever David had determined on as his course of action, his mind was made up and there was very little that anyone could do to change it.

'There's a few things that need to be done,' he said, 'before I'll be completely free.'

'There's something I think you need to know,' Caitlin said, 'before you do anything.'

It made David pause. 'What?' he enquired.

Caitlin told him of her conversation with Jenny. David listened while she repeated word for word what had been said between them. When Caitlin finished, David ran his fingertips along his jawline. 'That puts the seal on it,' he said. 'Thank you, Caitlin. I know exactly what to do.'

Caitlin couldn't suppress an internal quiver of dismay. She hadn't known Jenny well, but she had seemed a nice enough person. To believe that she had been Michael Crawley's informant somehow destroyed confidence in other human beings.

'What are you going to do?' she asked David.

'Ring Anderson, the accountant,' he said.

Caitlin's mind did a double-take. Of all the responses she thought David would make, this was one she had never contemplated. She picked up the phone, hit the automatic dialling, and waited until she was connected before she passed the instrument to David.

He sat on the edge of the desk, relaxed, self-confident, arrogant. 'Jeremy, this is David Hartley. I want you to drop everything you're doing, come over here, and run my business for a few days.'

Silence as he listened to the response.

'Jeremy, it's no good telling me this is an unreasonable expectation. I need you here until I can install a general manager.'

Caitlin's mind did a triple-take. What on earth did David think he was doing? Giving up the ground to Crawley? Distancing himself from some perceived danger? For David to pass over the reins of his business to someone else would be like cutting off his hands. It was so unlike anything she'd ever seen or heard or known of him that it felt as if the whole world was turning upside down.

'I know it will rip your schedule to pieces,' David was saying. 'What do you think has happened to my schedule? It's so ripped to pieces, there's no schedule left at all.'

Caitlin could hear the sound of the raised voice on the other end of the phone even from where she was sitting.

'It's no good getting excited, Jeremy,' David said smoothly. 'If you can't handle my needs, then I'll have to get a firm of accountants who can.'

The sound of the raised voice diminished.

'Dalhunty is the best in the field,' David said. 'He'll be the new general manager.'

A further pause.

'Jeremy, I don't think you understood what I told you. I didn't say I was trying to get Dalhunty. I already have him. He starts next Monday. You're deputising for me here until such time as Dalhunty commences.'

A much shorter pause.

'Thank you, Jeremy. I knew I would have your fullest co-operation. When you do get here in a couple of hours' time you'll find a few staff changes have been made. Simply carry on from there. I'd advise bringing your personal secretary with you.' His eyes targeted Caitlin with their magnetic power fully charged. 'My assistant will be accompanying me.'

David put the phone down.

Caitlin was now completely bewildered. 'What does this mean?'

'It means it's time to see Jenny. Would you call her and ask her to step up to the office, please, Caitlin?'

She did as he requested. 'What now?' Caitlin asked bleakly, feeling miserable for the young receptionist although accepting that the matter couldn't be overlooked.

'I think we should be as gentle as possible.'

'*We*?' Caitlin looked at David as if she had never seen him before. David had never said *we* at any other time. Before today it would have been *I*. His decision. He was linking himself to her, as if they had a common bond, a common purpose. Which led to the burning questions...where was he expecting her to accompany him? For how long? For what purpose?

Unfortunately there wasn't time to pursue the answers. They heard the elevator doors open and close. David called out, 'We're in Caitlin's office, Jenny. Please come in.'

She did. Caitlin realised that Jenny had opted for defiance in her own defence. She bristled like a porcupine. Her eyes flashed fire. Caitlin felt like burying her head in her hands. Defiance wouldn't get Jenny anywhere with David Hartley.

'Please sit down, Jenny,' he said, and brought her a chair. He did sound kindly disposed towards her, almost avuncular.

Jenny sat down. She folded her hands together in her lap, but did not lower her eyes. They followed every movement David made with punctilious care.

'You must feel very confused, Jenny,' David said quietly.

'Not one bit.'

'The reason I had a rule against the involvement of two of my employees in a relationship together,' David went on as if unaware of the acid in Jenny's voice, 'was to avoid the pain that so often follows office affairs.'

Jenny's face turned a rich scarlet. 'I'm not involved in any office affair,' she said stoutly.

'Of course not,' David replied, smoothing over the umbrage in Jenny's voice. 'It must therefore have been very confusing to you, and to others, when it appeared that I was breaking my own rule because of my...involvement...with Caitlin.'

Caitlin had to bite down on her tongue. She had not realised that David was about to plunge in and discuss their private concerns with anyone else at all. Why was he making a public confession of something that was intimate, personal and private?

There were so many changes going on this morning, her head was starting to whirl.

'It was obvious to everyone,' Jenny replied tartly.

'I'm sure it was,' David replied succinctly, 'and therefore confusing.'

'It didn't confuse me,' Jenny replied. 'It's what you expect from a *man*. They say one thing and do another.'

It was all too true, Caitlin thought. More than once she had reflected in the same way about the matter herself. Jenny might not be feeling confused, Caitlin thought, but she herself felt quite an urgent need to get several matters clarified.

'Caitlin and I were different,' David went on.

'Everyone thinks they're different,' Jenny pointed out with some asperity.

'Too true,' David said softly. 'And you thought you were different too, didn't you, Jenny?'

'What's that supposed to mean?' Jenny asked suspiciously.

'You had a lover,' David said. 'Someone else who was employed here.'

That was news to Caitlin. Who could it be? One of the salesmen? One of the factory hands?

'I'm afraid your lover is never going to marry you,' David said, his voice reflecting caring and concern. 'If he promised you that, Jenny, you're going to be very bitterly disappointed.'

'How can you possibly say that?' Jenny asked belligerently.

'Because he's already married.'

'He's not!' Jenny cried in vehement denial.

'Did you ever ring him at home?' David asked.

'No. Of course not. He's got a very sick mother. She can't be disturbed.'

David winced. 'Is that the reason he gave you?' he said, slowly shaking his head.

'That *is* the reason.' Jenny's hands started moving restlessly, fingers interweaving, scraping over knuckles. 'It has to be,' she declared.

'I'm afraid not, Jenny,' David said. 'I happen to be quite involved with the people who work for me. I like to know their backgrounds, what their aims and ambitions are, what little ways I might be able to find to help, at different times.' He rose to his feet, walked towards Jenny, tried to soothe and console. 'Paul Jordan has a wife and three children, Jenny. He was using you.'

Caitlin's mind flipped back to yesterday. She'd never liked Paul Jordan. He had certainly been aware of the St Valentine's Day gift when she arrived at work. Jenny had known, too. But it had been Paul Jordan who had played it up, making the comment about wishing her many lovers. The jigsaw started to fall into place in her mind.

'Yesterday, when you came into my office to look at the roses, you saw my letter of resignation on the desk, didn't you, Jenny?' she softly pressed.

'Why...why, yes,' she said defeatedly. She started to cry.

Caitlin had to ask one more question. 'And when Paul Jordan came back late in the afternoon you told him what you'd seen?'

Jenny nodded her head, too distressed now to speak any further.

Caitlin caught David's eyes.

'It had to be so,' he said quietly. 'It was the only thing that made sense.'

Jenny did not wait to be dismissed. She rose from the chair and blundered out of the office, sobbing as though her heart was broken. Caitlin followed her to the door and saw her running down the corridor to the ladies' room. There was nothing she could do to help. Jenny wasn't the first or the last woman to love foolishly, but that knowledge didn't ease the deep private pain of it.

Yesterday Caitlin had thought her own love for David Hartley was foolish. Maybe it still was, although David was certainly not married with three children. And the parameters of their affair were now changing, so fast that Caitlin had completely lost her bearings.

She turned back to David, thinking of the sensitivity he had just displayed. It made him more attractive than ever. 'What are you going to do about Jenny?' she asked.

'Probably nothing,' he answered. 'She was a pawn. She's been hurt enough. I don't think there's any need to do any more than what she's already done to herself.'

'What's next?'

'Paul Jordan,' he said, his voice hardening, and Caitlin knew the result for him would not be the same as it was for Jenny.

The salesman was summoned.

The conversation was short.

'You're finished here,' David said tersely to him. 'I have it in my power to break you financially and professionally. You have broken the duty of fidelity that you owe to this company. If you want to associate with scum like Crawley, then you're welcome. Remember this, though. Until the Statute of Limitations runs out in seven years, I hold your fate in my hands. That's near enough to twenty-five thousand days and I hope every one of those days you'll reflect on that.'

Jordan left a broken man.

Cold, hard and ruthless. That was what his competitors thought, Caitlin reflected. 'Are you going to take any further action against him?' she asked.

'No,' said David. 'To a man like Jordan, what he is about to go through is punishment enough.'

It also restricted the punishment to the man who deserved it. His wife and three children would not be innocent victims of his perfidy, provided, of course, Jordan could talk his way into another job. Caitlin admired David's restraint. In the circumstances, he could have been forgiven if he had taken a merciless course. People who saw him as cold, hard and ruthless were wrong.

'Where does that leave us?' Caitlin asked.

'As soon as Jeremy Anderson gets here, and I can brief him and hand the reins over,' he smiled at Caitlin, 'it leaves us with time on our hands to do the little essentials of life.'

The smile was enough to scramble her brains and send a surge of warmth through Caitlin, but she determinedly collected enough wits to find out what she needed to know. 'Spell that out specifically, David,' she said, trying her utmost to sound firm and in control of herself.

'I thought we'd already agreed.' The smile turned into what could only be called a wickedly tantalising grin. 'We have to buy a horse. And a nice little property to put it on.'

Caitlin took a deep breath, held it for a few moments before she released it. In a way nothing had changed. It was the same as when she'd first started working for him. When David started to move, it was always with breathtaking speed.

He wasn't promising her anything except a horse, she warned herself. If she went along with him, she would be dancing with the devil again.

But she couldn't help it.

She loved David Hartley and she had to give that love a chance to lead somewhere good.

CHAPTER THIRTEEN

'WHY can't you decide?' David was showing increasing signs of restlessness as he drove the Ferrari along the tortuous country roads.

'It's impossible to find a replacement for a horse like Dobbin on the spur of the moment,' Caitlin replied logically.

'We've looked at ponies. That took two days,' David reminded her. 'We looked at Galloways. That took the most part of one day. We've looked at Arabian horses and racing thoroughbreds.'

'I had Dobbin for thirteen years,' Caitlin said matter-of-factly.

'Do you think it will take that long to find an adequate replacement?' David sounded quite distraught.

'I won't know until I find one,' Caitlin said reasonably.

'It's very hard,' David muttered.

It wasn't that he was bored, Caitlin assured herself. What David found 'hard' was her insistence that there be no physical intimacy between them for at least one week. His stress level was rising with each succeeding day... six of them since they had last made love on the morning of St Valentine's Day.

Caitlin found it rather difficult, too. Still, she was not going to let on to David how much she missed and wanted that intimacy with him. In the last few days they had done a lot of talking. This not only helped to ward off the desire for more physical needs, it had given Caitlin a far more rounded and filled-in picture of David's life.

She now knew he was an only child. After many miscarriages his father had insisted that his mother give up trying for more children. He couldn't bear her to go through any more pain.

His father had made and sold quality furniture. Owing to the influx of cheaper mass produced furniture, his father's business had been on the verge of bankruptcy by the time David went to university to do an engineering degree. David had suggested revolutionising the business along the lines he later developed himself. His father had invested heavily in the change, but before it could begin to be profitable he had been killed in an industrial accident.

David had stepped in to rescue the situation. It was his responsibility to make the business viable. He not only owed it to his father, but his mother had to be provided for. That was all he would say upon the subject of his mother, but he had talked quite freely about the difficulties he'd faced and overcome along the road to his present success.

The more he revealed of himself, the closer Caitlin felt to him. She didn't want to resume an affair with him. Surely this idea of buying her a horse, as well as a property to put it on, meant more than that. Yet not once had he broached the subject of their future together in any concrete detail.

He had not asked her home with him to meet his mother. In that area, all forward progress was stalled.

'What are you thinking, Caitlin?' he asked.

'These are the times that test women's souls.'

'And other things besides,' David reminded her.

'It's not easy for me,' she reminded him.

'Nor me,' he semi-growled.

She knew what *he* was thinking.

What was happening between them was at Caitlin's insistence. It was all her fault. As soon as she changed her mind over artificial restraints on touching and feeling, life could return to normal. That was what David thought.

What David didn't know was that Caitlin wasn't going to change her mind. She remembered very clearly what had happened between them just after six o'clock on the morning of February the fourteenth. She didn't want David to ever lose that recollection, either. If Caitlin needed to be held, kissed and cuddled, then held, kissed and cuddled she was going to be.

Nevertheless, she was less and less sure that enforced restraint would achieve this desirable end. She struggled against the temptation he stirred inside her from merely a heated flash of his eyes.

'This is a procedural check,' she told him, 'on steadfastness, stick-at-ability, commitment, endurance, caring, ...'

'There are other things I would rather do,' David said, sounding a little testy, 'to demonstrate endurance, commitment, caring, stick-at-ability...'

'You must see more in me than physical union,' Caitlin interrupted archly. 'After all, you promised me a list. A long list. You gave me to believe that I had a large number of attributes that you found quite attractive apart from...'

'So true,' David asserted, but without optimum vigour. 'You must be aware, though, that you have a chemical reaction on me that makes my biology burn. I'm burning now,' he protested. 'I'm burning all the time. My biology is being incinerated. And I'm a reasonably young man. At this rate, I estimate there won't be anything left of me by the year...'

'Here's an interesting place,' Caitlin said in order to divert his attention from his burning.

David slowed the Ferrari down. He turned into the driveway.

'Featherstone,' she said. 'Nice name. Clydesdale stud. We'd better go and have a look, David.'

David needed all the distraction she could give him.

'What do we want with a Clydesdale stud?' he grunted.

'Satisfied curiosity,' she replied.

'Have I told you how beautiful you look today?' David asked.

'Eleven times,' Caitlin soothed.

'Maybe if you dressed yourself in something more ill-becoming,' he said, 'I wouldn't feel quite so teased, tantalised and severely tested.'

They were both wearing jeans, ordinary plain blue jeans. She had teamed hers with an embroidered peasant blouse which was quite pretty, but it hardly rated as the height of sexiness.

'Do you want me to look like a scarecrow?' she asked.

'I'm not sure what we're achieving with all this restraint,' David muttered.

The echo of her own doubts was disturbing. 'You're satisfying me,' Caitlin told him.

'Not the way I'd choose.'

With a little spurt on the accelerator that told Caitlin quite a lot about his frustration level, he drove the Ferrari up to the front door. Caitlin had no difficulty in interpreting that David's patience was wearing thin. She sighed. Maybe there was nothing more to achieve.

Yet there was no doubt that David's attitude to her had changed dramatically since that fateful morning nearly a week ago. Given time, perhaps, anything was possible.

To David's credit, he was affability itself when Mr Featherstone came to greet them. David explained they were interested in acquiring a horse, at this stage they were interested in Clydesdales, and Mr Featherstone led them down to the yards to show them his stallions and mares.

Caitlin had always thought Clydesdales were magnificent horses, certainly the most handsome of the draught breeds. They were descended from the great war horses that heavily armoured knights had ridden into battle. For centuries this tallest and heaviest and strongest group of horses had supplied the power for jobs that tractors and trucks did today, pulling ploughs, hauling freight, drawing carriages. They were still used on farms and for show purposes where modern technology was eschewed.

On Farm Day, at the Royal Easter Show in Sydney, where her father had always shown his Galloways, Caitlin had loved the grand parade, invariably led by a splendid team of Clydesdales pulling a huge wagon. Great skill and horsemanship were demanded to drive a top team of twelve. It was a disappearing art form.

Caitlin had never been close to them before, nowhere near as close as she was today. They were big horses, dauntingly big, fascinatingly big.

'That's Danny Boy,' Mr Featherstone pointed out with pride. 'He's got a big future. Only two years old and Supreme Champion at the last show.'

He was beautiful. A bay with a white patch on his stomach. He stood a majestic seventeen and a half hands high, going on eighteen, Caitlin estimated. He would continue to grow for another three years. He was as solid as the earth he stood on. Proud, majestic. A royal blood line. Above all else was the sheer *power* of the animal, for centuries harnessed to the well-being and advancement of civilisation.

The flowing white hair below the knee and the hock—feathers they were called—gave him such a smart appearance. Caitlin fell in love with him at first sight.

Mr Featherstone led on towards a yard which held some roans. Caitlin did not follow. David stayed beside her.

'Best piece of equine engineering I've seen,' David commented admiringly, nodding towards Danny Boy. 'From a scientific viewpoint, if you multiply the sine of the angle by the power co-efficient, the proportions of mass to...'

'He's perfect!' Caitlin breathed.

'What on earth for?' David could not have been more surprised.

Caitlin walked up to Danny Boy, and started to stroke his muzzle. He was docile to her touch. 'He suits me,' she said.

'What are you going to do with him?'

'I don't know.'

'Would you ride him?'

Caitlin ran her eye over his girth, the strength of his hind-quarters, along his back. She shook her head. 'No way. I don't like heights.'

Mr Featherstone came back to collect them. 'Danny Boy's not for sale,' he informed them.

'Is that so?' said David.

'That's so,' said the Clydesdale man, as sturdy as his horses.

'Well, let me see if I can change your mind,' David mused purposefully, warming to the task in hand.

A tingle ran down Caitlin's spine. David never knew when to let go once he set his mind on something. He probably didn't understand how owners felt about champion horses. Caitlin did. Her father would never sell Pride of Scotland, his champion Galloway stallion. Not, at least, without the purchaser paying in blood through every pore.

'He said he didn't want to sell,' Caitlin reminded David. She didn't want to be involved in any kind of scene. On the other hand, she couldn't help but feel the wellsprings of disappointment.

The next half-hour was a flurry of bid, counterbid, demurral, change of mind, change of heart, and overriding everything else was David's insistence that Caitlin should have what she wanted.

It got down to Danny Boy's love-life, who he was to be mated with and why. Caitlin switched off. Genetic breeding was all very well, but she knew what she would do. She would put Danny Boy in a huge paddock and let him choose for himself. Nature had a good track record in looking after these things without any interference by humans.

At last the sale was made. When they climbed back into the Ferrari, David was full of elation. 'I got what you wanted, Caitlin,' he said, 'and only paid three times as much as I should have had to.'

It didn't seem to bother him at all. Was he so desperate to get back into her bed that he thought this had to be a winning stroke?

'I've never been so embarrassed in all my life,' Caitlin said quite truthfully. 'You were dreadful, David. Absolutely dreadful.'

'What was I dreadful about?'

'You wouldn't take no for an answer. That poor horse is going to be so exhausted doing what the owner wants...'

'I wish I were that exhausted.'

He was totally unabashed. His eyes twinkled happy triumph at her. Maybe he thought he was at last getting somewhere. Something had been achieved!

Well, he still had some learning to do as far as Caitlin was concerned.

'Now all we need is a property,' he said with a satisfied air.

'I don't think I could go through it again,' Caitlin said weakly.

The Clydesdale stud farm was on the Calga plateau. David took the route down Bumble Hill to link up with the Yarramalong Road to Wyong.

He had already outlined his plan to Caitlin about buying a property in the Wyong district. It was in easy reach of Sydney, her father could keep an eye on the horse, and land was always a good investment in this area.

Land was also exorbitantly expensive in this area, Caitlin reflected as they drove on. It worried her. Was David in his right mind at the present moment? Would he pay *anything* to get the matter settled between them? To prove whatever he thought he had to prove? He had certainly ripped up his schedule and divested himself of his business concerns on her behalf. That showed an enormous commitment.

Caitlin grew more and more disturbed about the situation. She spotted The Last Retreat coming up. It offered some kind of resolution to her inner turmoil.

'Stop at the hotel, David.'

'What for?'

'I want you to book us a room.'

David shot her a piercing look. The Ferrari veered towards the edge of the road.

'Look where you're going! Keep your mind on what you're doing!' she hastily warned him.

He corrected the drift of the car before they ended up in the ditch. He forced himself to relax back in his seat. 'Caitlin,' he said quietly, 'the horse was not a bribe. I don't want you to do anything. I don't need to be paid off.'

'I want to be sure you're sane before you start buying a property,' she answered bluntly.

The Ferrari slowed down. David eased it into the hotel car park and brought it to a halt. He switched off the engine, then turned to her, his face serious, his eyes probing hers with urgent intensity.

'I'm perfectly sane, Caitlin. I don't need your body to work off some madness inside me. But I'd be lying if I said I didn't ache to make love. I do.'

'I do, too,' she confessed. 'And if we're here, I won't be thinking of Crawley knowing about it.'

His brow furrowed. 'Is that what's been worrying you?'

'He said he knew. Every time you made love to me. His words were "laying me".'

David winced. 'I wasn't *laying* you, Caitlin. I was *loving* you. Blindly and selfishly perhaps, but you were never what a man calls *a lay*. There is a difference, a big difference. If it takes a month or a year of celibacy to prove that to you, I'll do it.'

'No.' She shook her head and looked down at the wing of motel units. A week ago, David had followed her here. She hadn't known what to believe then. It was different now. He had more than amply proved she was special to him. The only question left was, how special? That wasn't something she could make happen. It had to come from him.

'I'm sorry about Crawley,' David said, his voice roughening. 'I should have known better, Caitlin. I regret, very much, that I didn't stand by you that night and throw the filthy scum out on his lying face.'

'It doesn't matter now,' she murmured.

'It matters to me. I failed you in the worst possible way. It made me take a long, hard look at myself, Caitlin. I didn't like what I saw.'

Was that why he had suddenly stepped away from his business? Changed his priorities?

His hand touched her face. Very gently he turned her head towards him. His eyes blazed with a turbulent mixture of concern and need.

'I've been trying to erase my mistakes, Caitlin,' he said gruffly.

'It's not done with money, David.' Her mind dictated the words. Her heart was torn with the desire to simply forget everything in the passion of coming together again.

'The money's irrelevant,' he said dismissively. 'I wanted to please you, Caitlin. To show you I'm not all take. I can give. And I'll give you all I can.'

Tears swam into her eyes. 'Go and get us a room, David,' she said huskily.

He looked uncertain. 'Are you sure, Caitlin? You're crying.'

She nodded. 'I'm just being over-emotional. It's been hard for me, too. Please go. I'll wait for you here.'

He leaned over and brushed his lips tenderly over hers. She felt his tension, knew he was barely restraining himself. 'I'll be as quick as I can,' he murmured, and left her.

Caitlin blinked the tears away. David wasn't promising her all she wanted, but she felt wrong about holding out on him any longer. Love wasn't a matter of barter. If it wasn't freely given, what was it worth? He needed her. She needed him.

She alighted from the car to wait for him. He wasn't long. He came striding towards her, so essentially male, strong, dynamic, and passionately involved with her. She moved to meet him. He didn't break stride. He scooped her to his side, his arm almost encircling her waist with possessive fervour.

'It's number three,' he said, the key to the unit held ready in his other hand.

She said nothing. Her heart had started to thump with almost painful wildness. She was intensely aware of his thigh brushing against hers.

'I'll tell you why you're special to me, Caitlin. You wanted a list. I'll tell you what's at the top.'

Caitlin looked at him inquisitively. She didn't know what was bringing on this flurry of words, whether they reflected the urgency of his desire or the deep well of his inner feelings.

'You are the essence of womanhood and femininity. You act coquettishly, but you're not a coquette. A coquette teases and tantalises for the pleasure of it. You tease, tantalise and satisfy for the pleasure of it.

'You surprise me continuously with your range of responses to situations. Unpredictable but always logical. No woman could give more in her infinite variety.

'You warm me, charm me, keep me smouldering. When the flames die down to embers you fan them into a roaring blaze once more. No other woman could suffice.

'A man *buys* a woman when he can get up and leave her without a pang or a single regret. That never has happened between us, Caitlin. It never will.

'When I hold you in my embrace, I know with a certainty that there can be no other woman. There is no other woman. There never will be any other woman.'

His breathing was ragged, his pulse erratic. It was as close to saying he loved her as it was possible to get without saying the words.

She kissed his neck. 'Would you mind repeating all that, David?'

'Fiend,' he said.

They reached the door of the unit. She pushed her thoughts away. They weren't important right now. David wanted her. She wanted him. Feeling again what they felt together was more important than anything else.

He used the key.

The door opened.

Caitlin did not hesitate.

It was another threshold to be crossed in her love for David Hartley.

She crossed it.

CHAPTER FOURTEEN

PERHAPS it was knowing he cared that made the difference. It seemed to Caitlin that everything meant so much more... the way David kissed her, touched her, held her. He seemed attuned to her every response, nurturing it, heightening it, pleasuring her with a slow, intense sensuality as though wanting to savour every moment of increasing intimacy with her.

Despite his earlier pent-up frustration, David displayed no sense of haste. It was as though he was discovering her again as he peeled her clothes from her body, pausing to caress and love each part of her he uncovered. If she had been a goddess she could not have felt more thoroughly worshipped.

Caitlin was too mesmerised, too enthralled by what he was doing to her to think of undressing him. When she was finally, tremulously naked, and she fumbled at the buttons on his shirt, he stopped her, sweeping her off her feet and laying her on the bed.

'I want to look at you, waiting for me to join you,' he said huskily. 'There's no more exciting sight in the world.'

Nor to her, watching him divest himself of clothes, feeling the anticipation swell inside her as his body emerged, taut with desire for her.

'Remember the first time you entered my office for the job interview?' David murmured.

'Yes. Very well.' It had been like entering an electric field, her whole body tingling as the man behind the desk rose to greet her, the most handsome, vital man she had ever met.

'I'd never felt anything like it,' he confessed. 'The hair on the back of my neck prickled. My heart kicked. Life was suddenly super-charged. When you spoke, your voice seemed to sing through my head. When I took your hand, the mere touch of you sent a fever through my blood. I had to have you, Caitlin.'

So that was the effect she had had on him ... an instant chemical reaction so strong that it consumed any consideration he might have given to other interviewees. Caitlin felt awed by the fact he had never felt it before, awed and elated. She *was* different from every other woman who'd been in his life. As he was different for her.

'Is it still like that?' she asked.

'More. It's hell not having you.'

A straight statement of fact, the truth of it burning in his eyes, burning into her heart, touching on the same truth for her. As he discarded his last piece of clothing, Caitlin swung herself off the bed and wrapped her arms around his waist, hugging the heat of his flesh to herself, feeling and revelling in the solid muscle-and-bone reality of the man she wanted and loved.

'It's hell without you, too, David,' she whispered, pressing feverish little kisses down his throat, along his collarbones.

'Caitlin...' It was a half-strangled cry of need. His hands skated down her back and clasped her to him. His chest expanded, crushing the pliant softness of her breasts, confining her movement.

'Let me love you, David, as you did me,' she softly pleaded, running her fingernails lightly down over his buttocks.

She felt the muscles tighten. He took a quick, shallow breath and eased his hold on her. The desire to pleasure him, to show him how beautiful he was to her, was like a fever in her blood. She could feel his sensitivity to her touch, the excitement rippling under his skin, the acute response to the intimacy of her mouth sliding over him, the tremor in his thighs...and it stirred a passion to make him feel more and more, to imprint not only his body but his soul with her love.

His hands writhed through her hair. He arched back. Then with an anguished groan he jack-knifed forward, picked her up and carried her to the bed. He drove himself inside her in a frenzy of need and she wildly welcomed the intense thrust of possession, goading him to reach as deeply within her as she hoped she had with him, wanting the searing sensation of his flesh pounding within hers, seeking the ultimate fulfilment of melding into one.

It came like a white-hot flash, engulfing her body, engulfing them both in a moment of ecstatic union, peaking to a pinnacle of utter perfection, completion, then slowly, slowly sliding into a trough of languorous sensuality that fed an almost insatiable passion for more and more pinnacles.

Their bodies were so sensitised that the merest caress effected arousal. David had only to close his mouth over her breast and softly draw on it to make her writhe with the sweet piercing pleasure that streamed through her. She had only to stroke the innerside of his thighs and his need for her stirred anew. The constant heat of their involvement in each other melted the hours away.

There was a blissful sense of belonging, a recognition of it in their eyes, a celebration of it in every kiss, an affirmation of it in each intimate connection. Even when exhaustion set in and the need for sustenance cried out to be met, they were reluctant to release each other from the intense togetherness they had shared.

'Do we have to go back to Sydney?' Caitlin asked, burrowing her head into the curve of his neck and shoulder, wishing this incredibly wonderful interlude could last forever but knowing it had to come to an end.

David didn't reply at once. He stroked her hair for several moments, clearly mulling the decision over in his mind. Then he cuddled her closer, and rubbed his cheek over the top of her head. 'No,' he murmured. 'We'll do whatever we want.'

They spent the night at The Last Retreat. All night. They had breakfast together the next morning. Caitlin was so happy she couldn't stop smiling. Her high spirits were infectious. David was more relaxed, more light-hearted, more ready to laugh than she had ever seen him.

Their hunt for precisely the right piece of land for Danny Boy turned into a delicious game as they bounced ideas off each other, building a picture of what would be absolutely idyllic. They not only needed good pasture for grazing, there had to be a creek or a big watering hole he could splash around in, the right amount of shade trees, solid fences, and it shouldn't be too lonely for him. This led to a discussion on the purchase of some mares as well. David was very eloquent on the subject of a stallion's needs.

Going back to Sydney was postponed indefinitely. David took Caitlin on a shopping spree, since their quest would obviously take a few days and they needed fresh clothes. They also bought a book on Clydesdales.

David clasped the concept of spontaneity to his soul.

They made love. They had fun together. The sun shone. They shared a joy in life they had never shared before. It was wonderful. David found out that the best Clydesdale mares should have a very feminine face. He couldn't believe it!

The dream property grew and grew. If they were going to buy some mares for Danny Boy, and the mares had foals, they would need stables and a feedbarn. They would also need a house because someone would have to live on the property and look after everything. An investment of this size demanded a good manager.

They finally found the perfect place. It not only had a house, but a workman's cottage, as well. David had no hesitation in buying it, despite the horrendous cost. 'The ideal country retreat,' he said. Caitlin could not help thinking he meant it for both of them, for the future they would share together.

They drove back to The Last Retreat and made love again. It was immensely satisfying, yet as they lay entwined together afterwards there was a twinge of sadness in knowing that the quest was over. It brought to an end—had to—this idyllic existence. David's real life was back in Sydney.

There was the Crawley patent infringement case coming up in court. That had to be attended to. And won. Then there was David's business. Although he had handed the reins of management to other people, he would have to keep an eye on it. No one knew it as well as he did. Last, but far from least, there was his mother.

David had called his mother to say he would be away for a few days, but he still had not talked about her to Caitlin. It was a gap in their togetherness that she desperately wanted filled. He had met her family, albeit not under the best of circumstances. Nevertheless, he had met them, and spoken of her father with liking and respect. Surely it was now time for her to meet his mother.

Caitlin lay with her head on his chest, her cheek over his heart. He must love her, she assured herself. He wouldn't have done everything he had if he didn't love her.

'Caitlin...'

'Mmh?'

'There's something I have to tell you,' he said, his voice strained with a complex range of emotions. 'And I don't know how you'll react.'

Caitlin's mind instantly switched to red alert. This had to be important, possibly critically important. 'Tell me,' she invited, aware of the slight acceleration of his heartbeat. She lay very still, listening more for the feeling behind his reply than the words themselves.

There was a long pause. Her own heartbeat quickened. Her instincts told her this was something very serious, something that could affect them very deeply.

'It's not so much a matter of telling, but of seeing.'

Pain. Sadness. Uncertainty. She waited for him to go on. She knew intuitively he was feeling his way through uncharted territory, or territory that contained so many deadly pitfalls that to safely negotiate past them took enormous care.

'My mother was very beautiful,' he said softly, wistfully. 'As beautiful as you are, Caitlin.'

She held her breath, acutely aware that he was approaching a highly sensitive area...Crawley's weapon against him...

'Her hair was thick and black and wavy. She always wore it long. She had smooth creamy skin. Thick eyelashes...'

Caitlin frowned. Why the past tense?

'My father never had eyes for any other woman. He adored her. And she loved him very much. Sometimes it made me feel excluded.'

Lonely most of his life . . .

'It must have been a good marriage,' Caitlin said wistfully.

'Yes. They were very happy together. They did everything together.'

His lips brushed warmly over her hair. Did he want that with her? Caitlin fiercely willed it to be so.

'Then one day there was a fire at the factory,' David said flatly.

The industrial accident that had killed his father? Caitlin barely suppressed a shudder. To die by fire . . .

'My father tried to save the designs for the new furniture. My designs. That was the tragedy, because I could have drawn them again.'

The pain of countless thoughts of 'if only' was in his voice. Caitlin remained silent. There was no balm she could give to that pain.

'There was an explosion,' David continued. 'Tins of varnish, they said afterwards. My father didn't have a chance but my mother tried to reach and rescue him. She ran into the flames. I don't think she stopped to think about what she was doing. A reflex action. She simply couldn't bear to lose him. Burning with the passion she felt . . . the fire enveloped her.'

His voice faded into brooding silence.

Horror speared through Caitlin's mind as she thought of why David had never invited her home with him, why he had spoken of his mother's beauty as belonging to the past.

'She was...rescued,' he went on. 'A brave act by a brave man from the factory, although, perhaps, a merciless one. The burns...it was hell on earth for her, Caitlin. Months and years of hell. No one should suffer like that. No one should have to live through it. And then the skin grafts...'

Caitlin frantically searched for something to say to David. There seemed to be no words that were remotely adequate. It must have been hell for him, too: the grief, the sense of futility and helplessness, the anguish of watching someone you loved suffer so terribly.

'I wish I'd been there for you, David,' she said impulsively. 'It must have been the loneliest torment...'

He said nothing for so long, Caitlin began to wish she'd held her tongue. Had it been an inane thing to say? Did he think she hadn't meant it?

'I did have someone, Caitlin,' he said, a bitter note in his voice. 'We had planned to marry once we gained our university degrees. She came with me to visit my mother...once. When she realised what a future with me would entail... She recoiled from the sight of my mother. I couldn't accept that. Marriage to me quickly lost its attraction.'

'Then she didn't love you,' Caitlin said fiercely. She pushed herself up to look directly into his eyes, her own burning with a conviction so strong it refused to acknowledge the wary reservation she saw. 'I'd stand by you through anything, David,' she declared passionately.

There was a flicker of hope, quickly quenched. 'It's easier to say that than to do it, Caitlin,' he said with a touch of harshness. 'My mother never leaves the house. For good reason. People recoil from the sight of her.'

'Whatever she looks like now, she's your mother, David,' Caitlin argued. 'I'd never turn my back on anyone who was hurt in my family.' *Not even Michelle!* 'Do you think I would do that to someone as important to you as your mother?'

He searched her eyes, wanting to believe but not quite able to bring himself to take that last ultimate step of trust.

'She must be one of the loneliest people in the world,' Caitlin said with soft sympathy.

'Yes. She's terribly isolated. Apart from me she's alone.'

Caitlin now understood why he had made such a rigid ritual of having breakfast with his mother every morning. Whatever turned up for him during the day—or night—at least his mother had that company to look forward to. It was a measure, a high measure of how much Caitlin meant to him that he had made this exception for her. She would willingly have staked her life that David had made no exception to his rule regarding his mother since the time of the accident.

'You should have told me, David,' she said seriously.

His mouth tilted with irony. 'It's not easy. I'm telling you now.'

'Will you let me meet her?'

He sobered, his eyes reflecting the torment of that decision. 'It would be an ordeal for her, Caitlin. Perhaps an ordeal for you, too. I think you should give it deep consideration before you...'

'No,' she interrupted firmly. 'I don't need to give it any further consideration at all. If I'm to be part of your life, David, don't shut me out of your mother's life.'

'Caitlin...' He winced and looked away. 'You don't know...what you may be letting yourself in for.'

'I do know. You've told me. And I'm not flinching away from it, David. Don't judge me,' she pleaded. 'Give me the chance to prove what I'm saying.'

His gaze slowly came back to hers and locked onto it with passionate intensity. 'You could hurt my mother very deeply. That's how Crawley was going to get at us, by using her disfigurement to cause further injury. Please be aware of that. The slightest rejection on your part...this isn't a game you can play. It's very real. Very painful. For my mother to...expose herself...to anyone...'

She placed her fingers over his lips, silencing him. 'Trust me, David,' she appealed softly. 'I promise you, I'll be worthy of your trust.' If it took every ounce of courage and backbone and strength of will she could lay claim to, she would cope with whatever she had to face and deal with.

'I'll have to talk to her...prepare her...'

'Then I guess we'd better go back to Sydney,' she said with a smile.

He touched her cheek. She could feel the yearning in his fingertips. 'I want it to turn out right, Caitlin.'

'So do I, David,' she said fervently. 'So do I.'

She had all the answers now. Her understanding of the man she loved was complete. It made her love him all the more. Yet there was this last step to take, a step that might founder on his mother's reaction to her. She could accept Mrs Hartley. No doubt of that. The burning question was whether Mrs Hartley would accept her.

Nothing was certain.

CHAPTER FIFTEEN

THE meeting with David's mother was set up for a week's time. Caitlin gave a lot of thought to how she would handle it. She didn't ask for any advice from David. He didn't offer it. She knew he was tense about the outcome but there was nothing she could do to ease that.

In the meantime, other recent sources of tension between them came to resolutions that neither David nor Caitlin could have foreseen.

They spent a day with Dalhunty at the Hartley building in Chatswood, assisting the new manager to a comprehensive understanding of current business dealings. There was a new receptionist. Jenny Ashton had resigned. That was not surprising, but the fax that came in from Herr Schmidt was.

David read it to Caitlin.

'Unaccustomed as we are to being treated in the highly original way we were treated, it is our collective wisdom that you are the man with whom we wish to do business. You represent the future of our mutual interests. Please send us a copy of your licensing contract.'

There was a PS attached to the fax.

'Please tell Fräulein Ross that her acting in the boardroom was sublime. We are aware of the trifling exaggeration that she introduced into the sales figures for the Sutherland contract. If she is ever in need of a job, there is not one member of the delegation who would not have her on his staff. Fräulein Ross was *magnificent*.'

David's eyes flashed with irony. 'In other words, they love you, they hate me, but they need us, and Crawley's no good to them.'

The reason for that was soon apparent. After the first day of the hearing of the court case, Michael Crawley skipped the country, leaving behind massive debts, much ill-will, and Paul Jordan out of a job.

Privately, Caitlin was relieved that Michael Crawley had removed himself from their lives. A term of imprisonment or a huge damages bill awarded against him would only have fed his malevolence towards them. This way he was no longer a time-bomb that might one day explode. Justice might not be served, but justice did not prevent innocent victims from being hurt.

David's mother was the innocent victim of other people's reactions to her superficial disfigurement. Probably no hurt was meant, yet the hurt given left deeper scars than anything else. Caitlin understood how much easier it must have been to withdraw into complete isolation. Yet if the rest of the world were blind, David's mother would be accepted in the same manner as any other person. That was the cruelty of it.

Caitlin resolved to be blind to anything but the person inside. And there was something else she could do, as well, something she knew from her own experience of loneliness.

The morning set aside for the meeting came. David had not spent the night with Caitlin. She knew he would be doing everything in his power to make everything turn out right, to soothe his mother's fears and give her all the assurances he could. Caitlin was acutely aware of how critical to their future this meeting was. At the end of it a choice would be made.

She dressed quietly in a black skirt and cream blouse. Her make-up was minimal. It seemed tactless to draw attention to her superficial attractions.

She left her apartment in good time to arrive at the house in Lane Cove at ten o'clock. She drove with concentrated care and attention. The last thing she needed was any kind of accident to delay her. She did not want to add to the tensions inherent in the situation by keeping David and his mother waiting. That would be unforgivable.

She was a few minutes early. She counted very slowly to ten before approaching the front door. It was important to look relaxed even though she was churning inside.

David appeared almost as soon as she had rung the doorbell. It was obvious that all was not well. He did not return her smile. His eyes skated over her in apprehensive appraisal and fastened on the basket she was holding.

'I brought your mother a gift,' Caitlin said in explanation.

He gave a slight shake of his head, as though he knew that wouldn't help, but he refrained from comment. 'Come in, Caitlin,' he said flatly, without a trace of favourable anticipation in his voice, more a resignation to seeing out the inevitable.

He led her into the lounge-room. Mrs Hartley was standing by a window, ostensibly looking out, her back turned to Caitlin's entrance. Her soft blonde hair looked perfectly natural and was styled to cover her neck. Her arms were folded in a self-protective hug.

'Mum, Caitlin's here,' David announced quietly.

No response, except a tightening hunch of her shoulders.

'Mrs Hartley, I've been so looking forward to this meeting,' Caitlin softly pleaded.

'I've told my son I wish him every happiness with you, Miss Ross,' came the tremulous reply. 'I mean that...with all my heart.'

'I have no doubt you do,' Caitlin replied.

'I can only spoil things for you.' It was said with dull certainty. 'It's best that you make a life without me.'

'That's not true, Mrs Hartley. It's not true for David and it's not true for me,' Caitlin pressed in urgent response.

'I'm sure you mean well, Miss Ross, but I know I can only be a source of embarrassment to you.

And to the children you and David might have. I don't want that.'

Caitlin's heart sank. David's mother was not rejecting her. She was rejecting herself.

'Mrs Hartley, I appreciate, very deeply, the sacrifice you're prepared to make, but I would like the chance to get to know you. David loves you very much...'

'I've been a burden on him for many years.' She shook her head. 'I should have died with his father. I wish I had.'

'Mum, please...' It was a cry of anguish from David. He moved to her side and turned her gently towards him. 'You're not being fair to Caitlin, Mum. Nor me.'

'Life isn't fair, David,' she said brokenly.

'No, it isn't,' he agreed. 'But you don't have to shut doors that open to you. Please...give it a chance, Mum.'

She bowed her head, shaking it with such an air of hopelessness that tears sprang to Caitlin's eyes.

David drew his mother into his arms. 'I can't leave you to yourself, Mum. It's no use asking it of me. I can't.' His eyes sought Caitlin's over his mother's head, begging her understanding, tortured with the conflict of two loves. 'It would haunt me for the rest of my life.'

Caitlin knew it was true. David might be ruthless in many ways, but he could never turn his back on his mother. He couldn't pretend she didn't exist. Neither could Caitlin.

She set the basket on the floor, lifted the lid and picked up the tiny puppy that was still curled in sleep. She cradled it in her hands as she moved forward, ignoring David's frown, hoping to break the agony of decision-making that was clouding all their futures.

'Mrs Hartley, I'm sorry that you'd rather not know me,' she said softly. 'I guess it's hard to trust good intentions when they've failed before. I know you must have a lot of lonely hours, so I brought you a companion you can talk to when David isn't here. Please ... would you take her?'

David obligingly stepped back to allow Caitlin to present her gift to his mother.

'If you'll just hold out your hands,' Caitlin urged, carefully keeping her gaze on the puppy she was offering. She didn't want David's mother to think she was trying to satisfy some morbid curiosity.

'What is it?' Her voice was strained, hesitant.

'A little Australian silky terrier. Six weeks old. She hasn't got a name yet, but I'm sure you can think of one.' Caitlin smiled down at the pup. 'She loves being loved. She demands care and affection and attention. She'll do just about anything to get it.'

A hand reached out tentatively to stroke the soft silky coat. The pup stirred, eyes alert, and turned to lick one of the stroking fingers.

'Oh!' It was a breath of surprise.

'Please take her. I got her for you. I used to have a pony to talk to whenever I was lonely. But a puppy's just as good and you can keep her in the house. She won't take up much room.'

Still there was a hesitation, but both hands were in front of her now and Caitlin bundled the pup into them. It wriggled in the changeover. David's mother quickly fumbled it to her chest. The pup, in search of more security, hastily scrabbled his way up her dress and nestled contentedly into the curve of her neck and shoulder.

Caitlin laughed with pleasure and lifted dancing green eyes, skating straight over the disfigured face and fastening directly on the startled blue gaze of David's mother. 'You see? She's taken to you already. I hope you don't mind holding her.'

'No...I...' She stopped, confused by Caitlin's failure to look away. She was taken aback at Caitlin's lack of reaction. 'I...it's...kind of you to do this for me.'

'I love animals. Did David tell you he bought me a horse?'

'No.'

'Then we need to tell you all about it.'

Mrs Hartley looked at her son, still bewildered by Caitlin's natural manner, her eyes full of questions.

'There's such a lot I have to tell you, Mum,' David said. 'Caitlin's pony was injured and had to be put down.' His hand slid over Caitlin's shoulder and gave it a squeeze. 'We bought her a Clydesdale to take its place.'

'His name is Danny Boy.' Caitlin lifted her hand and stroked it over David's. 'He's a two-year-old stallion and...'

She bubbled on, describing her horse and recounting precisely how dreadful David had been in pursuing the purchase, which he denied, insisting it was only his standard procedure. Caitlin then related their search for the right property, with helpful and amusing asides from David.

His mother stood watching them both, stroking the pup at her throat, not quite knowing what to make of what was happening but not walking away from it. Caitlin was privately assessing the work done by the cosmetic surgeons. It was very good. Both David and his mother remembered the beauty which had been destroyed, making the contrast appalling to them, but there was no cause for horror. Caitlin had no problem at all with what she saw.

'Come and sit down, Mum,' David urged. 'Caitlin had better tell you what to feed the pup.'

He steered her to an armchair. Caitlin picked up the basket and brought it over to show her the contents. She dropped on to her knees beside the armchair and lifted each item out in turn.

'I bought a feed-dish and a packet of cereal and a tin of dog-meat, but you'll find she'll soon want to eat whatever you're eating.' Caitlin smiled. 'Silky terriers always want to do everything their owners do. If you have chicken dinner, she'll want chicken dinner, on a plate the same as a human.'

Mrs Hartley's gaze lifted slowly to her son. 'David, would you make us some coffee, please?'

'Yes, of course.'

He left them together. Mrs Hartley lowered the pup to her lap. Caitlin fiercely hoped it did not mean her gift was about to be rejected.

'You must love my son very much.' The blue eyes were moist but did not waver from Caitlin's.

'I do.'

'I'm sorry. I was ... so ... afraid ...' She bit her lips and swallowed.

'You know ... the wonderful thing about dogs is that they always return the love they're given,' Caitlin said softly, giving the older woman time to regain her composure. 'They're the most devoted companions in the world.'

'You want me to have a companion?'

'For when we're not here.'

A wisp of a smile. 'It's you who is special. David was right about that.'

'Thank you for accepting me. It means more than I can say.'

'My dear ...' She looked down at the pup. 'So small,' she mused. But her mind was clearly on bigger issues.

By the time David returned with the coffee, an understanding had been forged. He watched them talk together, his eyes moving from one to the other with pleasure. When his mother took the pup out to the kitchen in case it needed a drink of milk, he whirled Caitlin into his arms and kissed her with such intensity that they were both in danger of the situation getting out of hand.

'You work miracles,' he said huskily.

Caitlin tried to catch her breath. 'What's this about the children we might have? I haven't said anything on the matter at all.'

'Sorry. A slip of the tongue.'

'David, you haven't told me you love me.'

'Caitlin, I'm a seething inferno of love for you!'

'We could run a procedural check to see how long you can last.'

His eyes blazed into hers. 'It's love. Definitely love. Nothing else. Forget biology. This is soul-sizzling love. This is mind-destroying love. It will last the rest of my life. You are the most wonderful, adorable, beautiful woman in the world. I'll never forget this day and what you did for my mother, Caitlin. Never! It's so...so...I love you.'

He kissed her again to express his feelings more adequately and eloquently. Caitlin had no difficulty in working out where this was leading to. She thought they should get married very soon.

CHAPTER SIXTEEN

THE day after her first meeting with Mrs Hartley, Caitlin received a call from her own mother.

As it happened, David was in her apartment, discussing marriage plans. When Caitlin heard her mother's voice, she had the satisfaction of knowing she could deliver one piece of happy news. Her mother, however, had more urgent matters on her mind.

'Caitlin, I've got problems with your father again.'

'What's he done?'

'He went up the street with twenty cents in his pocket, met a salesman he knew, and came home with a Ferrari. He expects me to pay for it.'

Caitlin burst out laughing.

'Caitlin, this is not a laughing matter. A Ferrari is a very expensive car. And what's the good of it? Your father is the slowest driver on the road. He never goes over sixty kilometres an hour. It's ridiculous! Michelle says it's ridiculous! Trevor says it's ridiculous!'

'Well, Dad bought the pick-up truck the year I was born. Maybe he needs a new vehicle. Perhaps with all that power under the bonnet he'll be able to keep up with the flow of traffic better than he can now. What does Dad say?'

'He's very stubborn. He says he wants to drive me around in a Ferrari. He says I would look good in it, and he'd be proud of me.'

'What's wrong with that, Mum? If Dad wants to show you off, why not let him? It sounds great!'

'Does it?' she said uncertainly.

'Absolutely. You would look good in a Ferrari. It would look really top class turning up at the wedding in a Ferrari.'

'What wedding?'

'My wedding. David and I are going to be married.'

'When?'

'About six months.'

'Six months?' David queried critically. 'I was thinking of two.'

'Be patient,' Caitlin reproved him sternly. 'I have to be satisfied that you're sure about what you're doing.'

She also wanted time to win Mrs Hartley's trust and confidence. She hoped to coax David's mother into meeting her parents, widening her world a little. It could not be done in days or weeks, but perhaps by the end of six months there could be many changes in perception.

'Well,' said her mother, stunned. She quickly recovered her voice. 'Well, I must say I didn't take to him at first, but he's very handsome. And your father thought highly of him. Not that your father understands these matters. And David is certainly very capable at organising things well. I hope you'll be very happy, Caitlin. As happy as your father and I.'

'Thanks, Mum. Two Ferraris at the wedding would look good, you know.'

'Yes. I think your father will have to have one, even if it does annoy Trevor and Michelle.' Her mother's voice fell to a doleful tone. 'Michelle is pregnant again. You know how she gets once she's pregnant.'

'Congratulate them both for me. I'll ring them, as well.'

'She won't be able to be your matron of honour at the wedding, Caitlin. I know you'll be disappointed at that.'

'What a shame!' Caitlin said, and crossed her fingers. 'David and I weren't planning a big wedding anyway.'

'We're not?' David asked, completely surprised.

'No, we're not,' Caitlin said very definitely.

David's mother might be persuaded to attend a small, intimate wedding. And from there...well, she could come to their country retreat for weekends and get introduced to the wonderful world of horses.

'You are going to be a proper bride,' her mother said anxiously.

'Yes, Mum. Now why don't you go and pay for Dad's Ferrari? He'll be so happy. Time is passing by. You might as well enjoy yourselves. Spend whatever you need on doing whatever you like.'

'You're right, Caitlin. It would make your father happy,' she said decisively. 'When will we be seeing you and David?'

'After we buy the ring. I'll let you know, Mum. Buying a ring is almost as difficult as buying a property.'

'I know that, dear.'

'Bye for now.' She put down the phone.

'An emerald, a sapphire or a diamond,' David mused. 'Emeralds match your eyes. Sapphires demonstrate your sparkle and fire. Diamonds are forever.'

Her eyes sparkled at him as they would forever. 'You've been redeemed in my mother's eyes. She thinks you are not totally bad.'

He laughed. 'An improvement on the thoughts of the German delegation.'

Caitlin slid her hands around his neck and swayed her body close to his. 'I used to think that loving you was like dancing with the devil.'

'Let me waltz you off your feet, my love,' he said, spinning her into the bedroom.

Some considerable time later, Caitlin finally got around to asking, 'David, what are you going to do now you're not running the business?'

'Develop new designs. I've been thinking about it for some time. I enjoy the creative side, Caitlin.'

'How am I going to help?'

'Trying out the furniture for repetitive strain injury.'

'Be serious.'

'I feel we should let things develop spontaneously for a while. No more schedules. Be ourselves. Do as we please.'

'We could take in a movie.'

'Go to a theatre.'

'Read a book.'

'Make love in the afternoon.'

'Now there's a thought.'

'Plan a wedding.'

'Buy a dog.'

They talked and planned together for hours. Caitlin realised that their sharing together, so different from what it had been in the beginning, was now boundless. It would go on for the rest of their lives.

Caitlin rested her head on David's chest, at ease with herself and him. She had found her soul-mate. The hours and days and weeks and months of loneliness were now over for her. David was her perfect partner in life.

On the most romantic day of the year, capture the thrill of falling in love all over again—with

Harlequin's

Bachelors

They're three sexy and *very single* men who run very special personal ads to find the women of their fantasies by Valentine's Day. These exciting, passion-filled stories are written by bestselling Harlequin authors.

Your Heart's Desire by Elise Title
Mr. Romance by Pamela Bauer
Sleepless in St. Louis by Tiffany White

Be sure not to miss Harlequin's Valentine Bachelors, available in February wherever Harlequin books are sold.

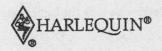 HARLEQUIN®

V

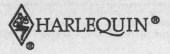

HARLEQUIN®

Don't miss these Harlequin favorites by some of our most
distinguished authors!
And now, you can receive a discount by ordering two or more titles!

HT#25577	WILD LIKE THE WIND by Janice Kaiser	$2.99	☐
HT#25589	THE RETURN OF CAINE O'HALLORAN by JoAnn Ross	$2.99	☐
HP#11626	THE SEDUCTION STAKES by Lindsay Armstrong	$2.99	☐
HP#11647	GIVE A MAN A BAD NAME by Roberta Leigh	$2.99	☐
HR#03293	THE MAN WHO CAME FOR CHRISTMAS by Bethany Campbell	$2.89	☐
HR#03308	RELATIVE VALUES by Jessica Steele	$2.89	☐
SR#70589	CANDY KISSES by Muriel Jensen	$3.50	☐
SR#70598	WEDDING INVITATION by Marisa Carroll	$3.50 U.S. $3.99 CAN.	☐
HI#22230	CACHE POOR by Margaret St. George	$2.99	☐
HAR#16515	NO ROOM AT THE INN by Linda Randall Wisdom	$3.50	☐
HAR#16520	THE ADVENTURESS by M.J. Rodgers	$3.50	☐
HS#28795	PIECES OF SKY by Marianne Willman	$3.99	☐
HS#28824	A WARRIOR'S WAY by Margaret Moore	$3.99 U.S. $4.50 CAN.	☐

(limited quantities available on certain titles)

	AMOUNT	$	
DEDUCT:	**10% DISCOUNT FOR 2+ BOOKS**	$	
ADD:	**POSTAGE & HANDLING**	$	
	($1.00 for one book, 50¢ for each additional)		
	APPLICABLE TAXES*	$_____	
	<u>**TOTAL PAYABLE**</u>	$_____	
	(check or money order—please do not send cash)		

To order, complete this form and send it, along with a check or money order for the
total above, payable to Harlequin Books, to: **In the U.S.:** 3010 Walden Avenue,
P.O. Box 9047, Buffalo, NY 14269-9047; **In Canada:** P.O. Box 613, Fort Erie, Ontario,
L2A 5X3.

Name: _____

Address: _____ City: _____

State/Prov.: _____ Zip/Postal Code: _____

*New York residents remit applicable sales taxes.
 Canadian residents remit applicable GST and provincial taxes.

HBACK-JM